SECRETS INBETWEEN

Pip Gorringe

ACKNOWLEDGEMENTS

Thank you to Verity, who kept pestering me to keep writing

Thank you to Grace, for guiding me through

Thank you to my daughter Bella, who is
my inspiration for everything

Thank you to my mum, Sue, who has had to read everything I've ever written and constantly told me 'this is your best work yet!'

And thank you to everyone who read my first few
chapters and encouraged me to carry on.

CHAPTER 1

Being bad at my job saved my life. Maybe you could put it down to laziness, or the fact I was addicted to my phone. Later on, I would be described as a beacon of hope and I would roll my eyes every time they said it. I wasn't a beacon of anything.

I had been in my new job as a theatre usher for all of 2 weeks. With no prior experience, I had practically begged them for the job during the interview. The chance to watch The Phantom of the Opera every night, to be a part of it, was a dream I could tick off my bucket list which I had made when I turned 18 and moved to London, just over a year ago. I had been assigned a locker to hold my things while I was working; they had a strict 'no phone' policy. Whether that was because it could go off in the theatre, or they were afraid we would film the performances, or they just didn't think we needed the distraction, I wasn't sure. All I knew is that I managed a total of three

days without my phone. On the fourth day I had pretty much learnt the ropes of the job and knew what I could and couldn't

get away with. By the end of my second week, due to what my grandmother referred to as an 'ample bosom' and the fact our uniforms had been designed with no pockets in mind, I had my phone safely secured in one side of my bra.

It was a Friday night performance, after the interval, that I slipped from the auditorium and made my way to the toilets. I settled down on a closed toilet seat lid and started playing candy crush with one hand, twirling a loose strand of blonde hair with the other. I had never thought I would think this: but there were only so many times one could listen to 'Down Once More'.

I had activated a particularly good special candy when I heard them. Bangs, maybe doors slamming or something louder. Then the shouting came, barked orders, muffled by the distance. I heard footsteps running down the stairs that went above me to the foyer. I let my hand drop to my side as I exited the toilet stall and paused by the bathroom door. Something wasn't right here. The banging continued and then the screaming began. I wrenched open the bathroom door and entered the bar area, which was eerily empty. I froze as the doors to the theatre stalls area opened with a bang and people came flooding out. No, not flooding – running. They ran towards me with horror in their eyes, some clinging to each other, some pushing others out of the way. That's when I saw him – or one of them. His face was concealed in a black ski mask and a black hoodie, the gun in his hands was something I'd only ever seen on films – but the way that he gunned people down was the most real thing I'd ever seen. He shot into the crowd almost lazily, taking no particular aim, nor needing to in the crowd of screaming, running, theatre goers. It was easy pickings. Horror filled me as I realised what was happening, or what was about to happen. As the ever-falling crowd reached me, I came to my senses and turned and ran to the stairs, upwards towards the foyer. *"Don't look back, Emily,"* I told myself as I ran, *"Don't look back."*

My feet pounded up the stairs, the vibration of my feet on each step shaking through my legs as adrenaline took over and I cursed my short legs. Other people were behind and to the side of me, I watched as they ran, scrambling to the top of the stairs. Some held hands with loved ones, my heart ached as I saw a man crying as he ran.

My foot hit someone behind me causing me to falter and the hand of a woman reached out to steady me as we carried on climbing. I managed a half terrified, half grateful smile as we reached the top and she gave my arm a brief squeeze as people separated us and she was carried off into the crowd. The scene in front of me made me stop as people pushed in front of me, the sounds of gun shots and screams not far below as the gunman picked his way through the crowd.

My colleagues were dead. Our security guards and doormen lay on the floor, like rag dolls in their own blood. The girls in the souvenir stand lay splatted on the ground and the box office door had been ripped off its hinges. I dreaded to think what or who lay inside. Bile rose in my throat as beads of sweat matted my hair to my head. They were all dead. I was shaken from my disbelief by the sound of metal rattling. I looked up to see that the metal security gate was down, the one we put down to secure the doors when we closed up for the night. The surviving crowd of people who had made it to the foyer were clawing and pulling at the gate, attempting to lift it up. I was the only one who knew it wouldn't be possible. Thinking fast I ran into the box office, the key for the gate would be in there. I stepped over the bodies of Dan and Ranjit with a cold detachment as I opened drawers that the key might be in. I had never locked up on my own, I had never been put in charge of the key. It was as I heard the bang of shots getting louder, closer, that I realised the gunmen would have locked the gate. They would have the key. I lifted my head to avoid looking at Dan and Ranjit's faces, both not much older than me. They didn't deserve this, no one did. Through the transparent box office screen, I could see the faces of people rushing past, some were bleeding, others screaming. People screamed other people's names, searching for their friends or family members. Some seemed to just be screaming at the impossibility of what was happening. I knew those screams would haunt me forever.

With my phone still clutched in my hand, Candy Crush still shone on the screen as I shakily clicked my phone app and dialled 999. This was something I had only ever done once before when I was very young and bored at my grandparents, my cousins and I daring each other to call and fake some emergency.

"999, what's your emergency?" A cool, calm voice responded.

"I need the police," I said hurriedly, my voice tripping over the words. The phone seemed to connect again and another calm voice responded.

"What is your location and emergency?" The operator asked.

"I'm at Her Majesty's Theatre in London. There's a man, maybe more. They're shooting everyone." I forced my voice to remain calm, but the screams were everywhere now and the rattling of the metal gate got louder. How could I even begin to describe what was happening here? Ice seemed to seep into my bones with every word. It didn't feel real.

"We're aware of the situation, the police are on their way." The calm voice responded, like milk trickling through honey. No accent, no panic, just smooth and calm. "Is there anywhere safe that you can hide?" She asked.

I looked wildly around the small box office with no door, I was a sitting duck here. I moved to the doorway. The foyer was now full of people, those closest to the metal gate were pulling and hitting it in a desperate and wild attempt to open it. I wanted to scream at them to stop, that it was a useless waste of energy, but perhaps they needed the hope. People were still coming from the stairs leading from the stalls and down from the upper circle. They must be everywhere. Exits sealed; they had thought this through. "There is nowhere safe." I whispered as the realisation dawned on me: I was going to die. We all were. A shiver went down my spine.

"If there is nowhere to hide, play dead." Said the calm voice as I watched a man reach the top of the foyer and fall dramatically as a smattering of blood exploded across his chest. The gunman had reached the foyer.

"Play dead?" I repeated, my voice void of emotion as the gunman reached the top of the stairs and started shooting wildly into the foyer. Was that a machine gun? I'd never seen one in real life, it looked like a prop from a movie, completely unreal.

People pushed past me to get into the box office to hide from him. It was only a temporary solution; of that I was sure.

"Yes, pretend you're already dead." Responded the operator, I had almost forgotten she was there. I let my hand fall from my ear as I pushed into the foyer and bullets shot around me, people fell with screams or grunts, writhing in pain. Another gunman, attire similar to the first, made his way into the foyer from the upper circle. More shots from downstairs made me realise I was right: there were even more of them.

I locked eyes with the first gunman, the only person frozen still in a room of running, screaming and writhing bodies. I couldn't feel my legs, all I could feel was the beating of my heart as it went into overdrive, blood rushed through my body and I felt like I was on fire. It was then that I fell.

I vaguely remembered a distant memory of being taught how to fall at drama class at school. Onto your knees, then to your bum, then onto your side. Gracefully and painlessly. All thoughts of that drama class disappeared from my mind as I fell face first onto the hard marble floor. Pain exploded in my head as it collided, a burst of warmth gathered around my head in an ooze of blood. I closed my eyes and urged myself not to squeeze close my shaking hands. I willed myself not to shake, not to move and not to breathe. *I'm dead.* I thought. *I'm dead, I'm dead, I'm dead.* I willed the gunmen to believe it too as I attempted shallow short breaths, my heart beating louder and louder. The screams around me were getting less and less and I tried not to react as someone fell against my legs, a body trapping me. I fought against the adrenaline surging through my body, urging me to fight or flight, as if doing nothing was not an option.

My body ached from the effort of keeping it still. It didn't seem long before the room grew silent, the smell of blood and sweat and fear thick in the air. All I heard was the squeak of the gunman's footsteps, sweeping through the room, dodging bodies, and looking for survivors.

I'm dead, I'm dead, I'm dead I thought over and over. I held my body still yet relaxed, remembering the bodies of my colleagues who were not far away. As the squeaking of their shoes got closer, I held my breath. *I'm dead* I thought. *Ignore me, I'm already dead.* The pool of blood below me had reached my lips, tickling my face. *I'm dead.* The pounding of my heart seemed deafening to me, giving me away. *I'm dead.* My mind started to fog as I battled with unconsciousness. Maybe it would be easier if I did pass out. I wouldn't be able to control my body or breathing, but I also wouldn't be able to feel anything. Maybe it would be easier if it were over.

"We've got a live one," I heard a gruff voice rumble nearby. My heart skipped a beat as a I heard a shuffle and a shot rang out. Then nothing. I desperately and internally checked if it was me, if I had been shot, but I felt nothing. The adrenaline in me saved me from having to feel the pain in my head. Perhaps I wouldn't feel my own death whether I was conscious or not. The squeaking shoes continued around the room. Every step they took made my teeth clench.

Still holding my breath, the floor beneath me seemed to give way as my unconsciousness threatened to take over. I took in a shallow breath as the sound of sirens approached outside. I would have cried with relief if my body thought it safe to move.

"Shoot the rest, just to make sure." Another low voice said quickly. "Then get the others." A grunt of agreement came from the upper circle stairs and a shower of bullets spread out around me. My battle with my conscious gave way. *I'm dead.* Then my mind went blank.

CHAPTER 2

I was stirred awake by someone gently touching my arm. "You're alive!" She whispered; her voice filled with wonder.

"No, I'm dead." I mumbled automatically, my brain fuzzy and my vision worse as I blinked and only saw a pool of almost dried blood. My head throbbed and my whole body felt numb, I tried to shift myself but couldn't make my body move.

"Stay down," She told me as I tried to move my head to look in her direction. Everything was dark and I could only make out her outline. When had the lights gone out?

"What happened?" I asked, my voice shaking. I knew what had happened, I knew exactly where I was and what was going on, but what happened after the shooting, I wasn't sure. The smell of death filled the room and I realised why I couldn't move. I was trapped. One body or maybe more lay across me, half covering me and pinning me to the spot.

"Stay still, it's not safe yet." She warned as I blinked a few times to make my eyes clear. I lifted my gaze to her and realised she looked familiar, but I wasn't sure how. Normal clothing: she wasn't a police officer or paramedic. Why was it not safe yet? She was up and about, and there was nothing more that I wanted right now than to get this body off me.

"Then you get down." I groaned as the ache in my head pounded, feeling as if it had its own heartbeat. I fought the need to throw up. My eyes darted around the room; all I could make out were the bodies on the floor. Nothing else moved. My eyes filled with tears. I was lying in a slaughterhouse.

"I'm... Fine. Just stay still and don't talk, it will all be over soon."

She gently stroked my arm to reassure me, and I realised how I recognized her. She was the women on the stairway, who had grabbed my arm to steady me as we ran up the stairs together. She must have found somewhere to hide that I hadn't thought of, or maybe she had played dead too. I wanted to ask but her warning was fresh in my mind and the stroke of my arm was reassuring and soothing. Soon my eye lids grew heavy again and though the ache in my head was stronger than ever, I drifted back into unconsciousness.

*

When I next woke up, I was in a hospital. My first thought was relief: a flood of relief so strong that tears sprung to my eyes and my body started shaking. I was safe, I was away from that place and I was safe, with machines bleeping around me and chatter of nurses nearby.

Then I remembered. The blood, the running, the fear. The sudden memory of everyone screaming and dying around me. I shot up and managed to turn my head before vomiting all over the floor. I groaned as my body shook and convulsed with every gag. Image after image running through my mind like a movie montage.

A nurse came running over with a disposable sick bowl, but it was too late, I was done.

"Here, take this," She said handing me a tissue and a plastic cup of water.

"Thanks." I rasped and wiped my mouth; my hand shook as I took a sip. "I'm so sorry." I apologised and eyed the vomit on the floor distastefully.

She smirked and shrugged "I've seen a lot worse. I'll go get someone to clean it up. Sit tight." She told me and exited the room.

I looked around the hospital room: large, with six beds in total, but I was the only one here. I found the control on the side of my bed and pushed the button to make the bed upright. I gingerly examined myself. I was out of my uniform and in a soft plain nightie. I gently fingered my sore forehead. It felt like I had stitches, but they didn't seem to hurt much. As I examined myself, a small girl wandered into the room. She was dressed in red and clutched a bundle of crayons in her hand.

"Hi," I said curiously. She jumped as though I had startled her and dropped a few of her crayons. She turned to face me, a little alarmed. "Sorry, I didn't mean to scare you, is this your room too?" I asked slowly, thinking it was odd, wouldn't there be a children's ward? Had my small stature made them mistake me for a child?

"You're alive." She told me, her face changing from shock to curiosity as she tilted her head and examined me. She couldn't be older than 7, but her eyes looked straight through me and there seemed to be wisdom in those eyes.

"That's what they keep telling me," I replied with a half-smile. She straightened her head but eyed me suspiciously.

"This is one of my rooms." She answered, glancing at the other beds. "There are usually more people." She shrugged, sounding nonchalant. She stepped closer to my bed and I could see the perfect curls of blonde hair that framed her face in detail, like an old china doll I had seen in films.

"Are you visiting someone?" I asked, curious as to what she meant. She shook her head.

"Not anymore." She responded. I nodded and looked away, confused. For some reason talking to the child felt draining and by judging from the sun in the sky, I must have slept all night. A wave of tiredness swept over me as wondered how I could be so tired after sleeping for so long. I stifled a yawn but the girl still saw and smiled at me. "I'm Rebecca." The girl introduced herself, her blue eyes mirroring my own.

"I'm Emily," I told her, smiling back and leaning my head back to rest it on the bed.

"Your hair is red." She stated, eyeing my hair as I had hers.

"No, it's blonde, like yours." I corrected, shaking my head softly and regretting it instantly as a shot of pain came from my forehead. Automatically I reached up to touch my hair and felt the crunch of dried blood. Well, at least I hadn't been bathed while I was unconscious. "It's just dried blood." I reassured her as I realised why she had been so scared when she first saw me; I must look like something from a horror movie, which perhaps wasn't far from the truth. The girl nodded, seemingly unfazed and glanced back towards the door.

"I have to go look at the other rooms now." She told me and headed back towards the door without making a sound. I nodded slowly as I watched the girl leave. What an odd child. Was anyone just able to wander in and out of hospital rooms whenever they wanted?

She had been gone for only a moment when I realised she'd left her dropped crayons behind on the floor. "Wait!" I called out as I jumped out of bed, the side with no sick on, and ignored the throb in my head. I walked into to the middle of the room and searched the floor with my eyes but couldn't see the crayons. I carefully knelt on the hard floor to look under the nearest beds, but nothing was there. I turned slowly, scanning the room. Had she picked them up without me noticing?

"Feeling better?" The nurse asked as she entered the room, watching me with laughing eyes as I knelt on the floor. Feeling foolish I stood up slowly.

"Yes sorry, I was just looking for... something." I paused, giving the floor one more once over then heading back to my bed. Perhaps she hadn't dropped any after all.

A cleaner followed shortly with a trolley of cleaning products and got to work on cleaning the floor. "I need to call my mum." I stated, looking at the nurse. My phone was probably still at the theatre. An image of my phone, covered in blood and hidden beneath bodies, danced through my mind while bile rose in my throat.

"We think there is someone downstairs for you, we just need to ask you some questions first." She paused as she saw the look on my face. I couldn't answer questions just yet, I had barely let myself think about what had happened. "No, not about that." She answered the unasked question quickly. "I need you to confirm your full name and date of birth. You were wearing your work uniform which had a name tag on, but we didn't have any information about you working for the theatre, we weren't sure exactly who you were." Her cheerful demeanour dimmed a little.

"I haven't been there long; I was still in my trial period." I told her, my mind flashing back to skiving in the toilet stalls. "My name is Emily Anderson, I'm 19." I answered automatically and stated my date of birth for clarification. All night I had laid in this bed and they had no confirmation of who I was.

The nurse nodded at me and smiled. "Your mum is downstairs." She told me. Of course, it had been hours since the… incident at the theatre, it would have been on the news. Mum would have jumped in the car in her pyjamas and no bag and started the 2-hour journey down from Birmingham before they had even finished the news story.

"Is she allowed up?" I asked, wondering why she wasn't here, next to me.

The nurse flashed a brief smile. "Yes, now that we know who you are. Your mum was insisting that it was you, but because we couldn't prove it and we've had a few journalists insist similar we had to wait for you to confirm to be sure." She nodded. She seemed glad, perhaps because she would be able to tell my mum that it was indeed her daughter who was upstairs, recovering.

I tilted my head as I digested what she had said. "You've had journalists lie before to try to see patients?" I queried.

"No," She responded. "We've had journalists lying to try to see *you*."

My eyes narrowed in a mixture of confusion and disbelief. "How about the other survivors? Why not them?" I asked, remembering the woman who had caught my arm and reassured me later, telling me to keep still. I wondered if she had family waiting for her downstairs, or whether she had already been discharged.

The nurse's eyes flashed up; all traces of her smile gone. She waited as the cleaner finished up and left the room with a nod, then perched at the end of my bed. She hesitated for a moment, her eyes briefly flashing up to my forehead.

"I'm sorry Emily but… There were no other survivors. You were the only one."

CHAPTER 3

I let the information sink in as the nurse left to fetch my mother. The theatre seated over 1,000 people, and though it hadn't been a full house that night, it wasn't far off. Then there was the cast, the backstage crew and the theatre staff. How could it be that every single one of those had been killed? How was it that I could be the only one who survived? How about the woman who had stroked her arm and told her to keep still? Had she slipped out without anyone seeing? Without noticing I shook my head in disbelief and my forehead shot out a wave of pain as a warning. Not having time to delve deeper into my thoughts, I was tackled into an embrace by a forty-year-old, tall, blonde women who would share a likeness to myself if she wasn't wearing make-up.

"Emily, thank goodness," My mother wept as she held me in her arms. I wrapped my arms around her and noticed the nurse step out to give us some privacy. I detached myself from my mother as she held me at arm's length, scanning my forehead. "They've said you should be able to go home this evening. After a shower and some food. They were worried about concussion, but scans have come back clear and I think they're less concerned now." She said softly, as if talking too loudly might startle me. I nodded slowly.

"What's in the bag?" I asked eyeing up the bag she'd thrown on the floor before embracing me.

"Oh, I bought some clothes from the gift shop, I hadn't thought to bring anything with me and thought you might need something." I smiled, knowing my mother all too well.

"Have you been here all night?" I asked, wondering how long she had spent pacing the waiting room, waiting for confirmation that her daughter was alive.

"All night and all day, it's almost dinner time." She responded nodding at the clock above the door that I hadn't noticed. Had I really been asleep for that long? "They wouldn't let me up until they could confirm it was you, they couldn't find your details. I told them you hadn't been working there long." I noticed how she paused before the word 'there' as if saying the word 'theatre' might trigger me. I realised, at some point, I was going to have to re-live it all. The thought filled me with dread.

"Don't worry, it's fine, I've been sleeping mostly." I shrugged it off. "How many stitches are there?" I asked, wanting to avoid the real topic of conversation.

"Only six. They said they don't think it'll scar badly." She confirmed, I hadn't even thought about it scarring, I suppose it seemed trivial really. "Emily…" Mum started and paused, a look of concern on her face.

"I'm ok Mum," I stated before she could continue. "I… Don't want to talk about it, but I'm ok." I finished, trying to give her a reassuring smile. If there was anything my body didn't want to do right now, it was to smile. Mum nodded and smiled back.

"Let's get you showered then, if you think you're up to it?" She asked. Gingerly I stood up and let her lead me to the shower whilst she went to get a towel.

The rest of the afternoon passed in a haze, the nurse came back to ask more questions and mum filled out some forms. I felt better having showered and with fresh clothes on. There had been no shoes at the gift shop, so I walked around in fluffy slippers which were a bit too big for my feet and I had to shuffle them against the floor to keep them on.

When I was finally released, they had to let me out of a rear staff entrance so to avoid any journalists that may still be hanging about. Mum insisted on taking me back to Birmingham with her for a few days but we decided to stop by my flat so I could pick up some things from my flat before we left.

"Any chance anyone gave you my phone?" I asked as she handed me my bag with my keys in it, which had been stored in the locker at the theatre.

"No, they said that this was all that was in your locker." She informed me.

"I know, I had my phone with me when… it happened. I called 999; my phone will be on the floor somewhere." Reluctant to say more I put the key into the door and pushed it open, relieved that it seemed none of my flatmates were home. Perhaps I wouldn't want that phone back anyway.

"So, you were the one to call it in?" Mum asked hesitantly, grabbing at the piece of information I had given her.

I shook my head quickly. "No, they were already aware of the situation by the time I called them. I don't know who called first." I responded, making my way into my bedroom and grabbing a small pink suitcase that was stored underneath my bed. "They… Told me to play dead. The operator." I confirmed, trying not to make eye contact as I saw the expression on her face, a mixture of horror and fear.

After a moment mum responded. "So that's what you did? That's why they didn't…" She paused, either unable to find the words or not wanting to.

"Yes, I think so," I said quickly as I gathered up clothes and assorted pieces of underwear. I wanted to pack and leave before any flatmates tried to accost me. It was hard enough speaking to my own mother.

"I spoke to the police back in the hospital, while you were in the shower." Mum told me abruptly as I was closing my suitcase. "They want to speak to you at the station. I asked them to give us some time, but as you're the only witness, they've said they have to have a chance to speak to you, before anyone else does."

I pondered this while I changed the gift store clothes for my actual clothes and found some slip-on trainers. "It's fine, I should probably get it over with. I need to understand some things as well." I told her as we headed back out the door.

The police station was busy on a Saturday night. Mum asked for some officer or other and I was led into a cosy room with sofas and a tv. I asked mum to stay behind, she hesitated and I couldn't decide if her reluctance was due to concern or curiosity but she nodded and I sat with two officers whilst another stood in the corner, like a silent security guard. The officer in front of me spoke while the other took notes.

"I want to be clear before we begin." Officer Jenkins started, "That we're not asking for a witness statement. I want you to know that all 15 terrorists were caught and killed last night." He waited to let the information sink in. There had been 15? It seemed like a lot. "By the time we got there, they were waiting for us and didn't want to go without a fight. This is public knowledge now." He confirmed, trying to gauge my reaction. I said nothing. "We have the security footage and though it's still being re-reviewed by a team of experts, we are sure that none of them escaped." I let out a small sigh of relief.

"Did anyone else escape? Victims, I mean." I asked gingerly. Slowly, Officer Jenkins shook his head.

"I can confirm that you were the only survivor that night." He stated sadly.

"They... erm, they shot everyone again, after they were down, to make sure they were dead." I stated. He nodded as if he was already aware of this. He'd probably seen it all on the security footage. He probably had to sit there and watch it all happen, from the moment they entered the building, to quickly and effortlessly securing the exits to make sure that it became a slaughterhouse with no escape.

"You have to be aware, Miss Anderson, that a lot of people will want to talk to you. A lot of people will have questions and will want to hear your side of the story. All I can say is that that will be up to you. How much you want to say and how you want to say it. I just wanted to make you aware that a lot of people have lost their family members and a lot of people will be asking why you survived when others didn't." A hot flame of anger flickered in my stomach. Did he think I didn't know that people would be asking that? That people had died and that not just London, but the whole of the UK would be in mourning right now? The only reason there weren't journalists at my front door was because there were no details on who exactly the only survivor had been.

Calmly I swallowed my anger. "I'm aware of the seriousness of this situation and I won't be talking to anyone." I confirmed slowly.

"That's not what I'm asking of you here." He responded quickly. I only nodded; I knew exactly what he was asking. No matter what I said, people would be upset.

"There was a woman," I started, deciding to ask my question before this could be derailed. "She was in the theatre. She helped me climb the stairs when it all started happening. Later, when everything was quiet, she was still alive. She spoke to me and told me to keep still, that it was almost over." I let the words rush out of me, if there was any hope that she could still be alive, that selfishly I wouldn't be in this alone, I had to ask. "It'll be on the security footage; can you tell me what happened to her?"

Officer Jenkins paused and exchanged a glance with the officer sitting next to him. "We've reviewed the footage Miss Anderson, after you fell there were only a handful of people left and once they were shot it was only the terrorists remaining. Once they left the foyer, they went to the stage to greet us. The only person alive in the foyer was you." He confirmed. I shook my head.

"No, I passed out and when I came around the first time I was still in the foyer and she was there, she was standing and talking and moving. Maybe she went around to check if anyone else was still alive?" I asked, almost desperately, they must have got it wrong.

Officer Jenkins paused with a mixture of concern and pity on his face. "I'm sorry Miss Anderson, but the footage has been reviewed quite thoroughly. I'm afraid that no one spoke to you after you fell. The first people back in foyer were my team and a team of paramedics."

I leant back on the sofa as I absorbed this information. Was it possible that I had dreamt her? I had been unconscious and lost a lot of blood. But her words and the touch of her hand on my arm had been as real as the gunman shooting around us. I nodded once to let him know that I understood. The memory of the girl in red and her disappearing crayons flashed through my mind.

Officer Jenkins spoke some more, helping me understand what had happened that night and why it happened, he told me the name of the terrorist group and that they were looking into other people who could be a part of it. He told me how brave I was, but he explained that unfortunately he couldn't get my phone back to me; there were a lot of possessions on the ground that night and it was all forensic evidence. I barely took in the words that he was saying as my mind whirled to try to figure out exactly what was happening to me and what it all meant.

As we stood up, I shook both their hands and thanked them for their time. I looked in the direction of the silent third officer who had been guarding the door. "Thank you." I nodded at him. He gave me a smile and a wink as Officer Jenkins exchanged a quizzical look with his colleague.

"You're welcome, again." Jenkins said as he opened the door.

"Oh no, I meant him," I said gesturing towards the third officer, who had stepped into the middle of the room to let us pass. Jenkins exchanged another look with his colleague who had been taking notes.

"Who?" He asked. My eyebrows furrowed and I turned to point at the third officer, but he was gone.

CHAPTER 4

On the way back to Birmingham I filled mum in with the details of what had happened at the police station, leaving out the parts about the woman who had stroked my arm and the disappearing police officer. I had managed to choke down my surprise, laugh it off and quickly leave the room. There had only been one door and we were standing in front of it, unless he had quickly hidden behind the sofa for some weird, elaborate joke, he had definitely disappeared into thin air. If I hadn't just been through what I had in the last 24 hours, then I would probably be a shaking mess. Perhaps there was a silver lining to all this: perhaps I was stronger for it.

I told mum about the terrorists: how it had been a hate crime formed by a larger group that they were now investigating. The drive up to Birmingham was uneventful and I tried not to drift off; every time I closed my eyes, I saw a mixture of the kind woman, the little girl in red and the policeman that had disappeared. When we arrived, mum carried in my bag as I slowly approached my childhood home. It was a modest two bedroom semi-detached in a town on the outskirts of Birmingham. It had only been me and mum in it since I was born. My dad left my mum before she had even known she was pregnant. I'd had good memories here and though it was hard to leave mum for London when I was 18, she had encouraged me to follow my heart and go on adventures, but this place would always be home for me.

"Cup of tea?" Mum asked as she clicked down the knob on the kettle. I shook my head. Tea meant a conversation which I wasn't ready to have. I had so much more in my head that I had to work through.

"I'm just going to head to bed if that's alright?" I asked, surprised how tired I was after sleeping roughly 17 hours. With just a glance of concern she nodded, and I made my way up the stairs to my old bedroom. My bedroom had remained exactly the same as when I left it after my last visit, which was roughly a month ago. I traded my clothes for comfy PJs and flopped on my bed without unpacking my suitcase. I didn't know how long I would be here, but the police had told me my identity would be released to the press in the morning and my flat might be bombarded with journalists. I should have probably warned my flatmates, but without a phone it would be near on impossible at this point. I wrapped my blanket around me as I closed my eyes, deciding to work through the events of the last 24 hours. I knew I wouldn't be able to come to terms with it overnight but I had to figure out what it all meant to me, but before I had the chance, I drifted into sleep, exhausted from the day's events.

I woke to the sounds of screams filling my ears. I sat bolt upright but it was a moment before the screaming faded and I realised I had been dreaming. My bed was damp with sweat and as I climbed out, the trace of a memory from the dream was beginning to fade. I took a deep breath and dressed silently, whilst surveying myself in the mirror. The stitches were neat and even across the top of my forehead. For the first time in my life I considered cutting in a fringe just to cover them, so I would not have a daily reminder of what had happened to me, staring me back in the mirror. Deciding to wrench myself away from the mirror before I made a big mistake, I wandered downstairs and absentmindedly switched on the tv and regretted it almost instantly. A picture of my face flashed up on the screen – my profile picture from Facebook of me posing and staring off into the distance, looking thoughtful. Headlines flashed underneath it, the only survivor of the terrorist attack on Her Majesty's Theatre. I looked younger than I felt. 1,106 killed that night, including all the attackers. Other names flashed up on the screen, Mark Hilbert, who had tackled one of the terrorists before being shot.

He would be known as a hero. Sarah Ryan, the youngest person there who had only been 11 years old. Brian Philips, a crew member who had seen the first attacker enter backstage, who hid and called for the police. Bile rose in my throat as I switched the TV off. They were all heroes in my eyes. All I had done was play dead and was lucky that no stray bullets had reached me. What if I had told others in the foyer? What if I had grabbed at least one person and whispered in their ear to play dead too. Would they be alive now? Had anyone else attempted to do what I had done, maybe in the stalls or the actors on stage? How was it possible that not one of them had survived this, other than me?

Swapping my slippers for my trainers and grabbing a hoodie and my keys, I slipped out of the house. I let my legs wander down my cul-de-sac without having a destination as I shifted through my thoughts. The woman who had stroked my arm hadn't really stroked my arm; she hadn't been there. She had been dead. Was she really just a figment of my imagination, my mind concocting a vision of the last kind face I had seen, to reassure myself? I tried to rationalise it in my mind. How about the strange girl in red, who seemed neither patient nor visitor and her disappearing crayons? Or the policeman that had disappeared practically right in front of my eyes? Was I so traumatised by this experience that my mind was playing tricks on me, seeing things that weren't really there?

I didn't know whether to talk to someone about it, whether it would go away on its own, or whether I'd be called crazy. I stopped and took in my surroundings; I had ventured into our local park which spanned over 2,400 acres and was actually one of the biggest urban parks in the UK. I wandered down the familiar paths and took in the early morning summer warmth on my face. How many people were meant to be waking up right now, that would never wake again?

"Penny for your thoughts?" A voice came from the shadows of

nearby trees.

Startled, I turned around wildly, looking for the face to match the voice. "Hello?" I called out hesitantly as a man stepped out, the early morning sun giving him a halo of warmth that seemed to surround his body like a fine mist.

"I apologise, I had not meant to startle you, you just looked so deep in thought, I could not help but be curious." He smiled and took another step closer, he was dressed smart for a weekend, with a shirt buttoned to his throat.

I eyed him suspiciously, wanting to roll my eyes as the description 'tall dark and handsome' sprang to mind. His tanned skin and dark hair made me wonder if he could be Spanish, or Greek perhaps, but his accent was very clearly English, almost aristocratic. "It's fine," I answered, lying. I was in no mood for company, no matter how good looking.

"You are glowing, did you know that?" He asked, his amber eyes shone bright in the morning sun, attempting to entrance me.

My eyebrows wrinkled as I frowned. "Does that pick-up line always work for you?" I laughed off the compliment and started walking back up the path, very aware of how alone I was and without a phone. In the corner of my eye I saw him fall in step behind me.

"It is why I followed you." He responded from behind me. I froze and turned slowly. Could I outrun him?

"Followed me?" I tried to laugh as my mind whirled. How far had I wandered down the path? How quick could I run before he could reach me? How stupid could I be to wander into the park early on a Sunday morning, with no one around and no way to reach for help?

"Do not be alarmed." He responded reassuringly, watching my panic rise. "I saw you in London, but I wanted a chance to approach you on your own." He lifted an open hand, perhaps a gesture to show he was unarmed, but his gentle manner and soothing voice did nothing to calm me.

My heart skipped a beat as I digested what he'd said. London? He had followed me all the way from London? "Look, I'm not sure what your deal is but my mum is just down the path and she's quite happy to kick the ass of any man that looks at me twice, let alone follows me, so I'll be going now." I stated curtly, tucking my hands into my hoodie's pocket, I turned and began to walk briskly away, trying to look more confident than I felt.

I heard him laugh behind me, it was a lovely, gentle laugh, like liquid silk. "We will meet again Emily." I heard him say gently, but his voice seemed to be closer now, much closer than before. I took my hands out of my pockets and began to run.

CHAPTER 5

I stopped running when I came to the gate that lead to the road, partly because I felt safer and partly because I couldn't breathe. Running had never been my strong point. At sports day I had always opted for the relay race, because it was the shortest amount of time that I would have to run for. I went through the gate and glanced behind me quickly to make sure he wasn't close behind. The path seemed clear. I rested my hands on my legs and stood bent over for a few moments while I got my breath back and decided whether I was going to pass out or not. The moment passed and the fear began to fade as cars went by and the chatter of nearby people reached me. I straightened up and headed down the road that led to my house. I decided that, much like the other strange people I had encountered recently, I would also be keeping this to myself. And no more lone trips to the park early in the morning.

Mum was still asleep when I got home and didn't appear until after I'd eaten breakfast.

"I had Nicki message me on Facebook; she's coming over today." Mum blurted out before she could change her mind. "How are you feeling today?" She asked, nodding at my forehead.

"Fine," I answered shortly, guilt welling up inside me from the lie and all the unspoken truths. "I bet Nicki is going crazy." I almost laughed. Nicki had been my best friend since I was in primary school. She was completely wild and fierce and everything I wish I had the guts to be. Last year, I decided to move to London and she had decided to travel the world, with nothing but a backpack and the small inheritance her grandmother had left her. Never staying in one place for more than a few days, she saw more in a year than most people had in their entire lifetimes. When she got back, she had stayed with me for a few weeks in London and we spent most of it catching up properly,

eating junk food and gossiping about boys, like old times. Second to my mum, she was the one person I could trust, and I would bet anything she was going stir crazy hearing what had happened and not seeing me.

"She certainly is," My mum responded, putting on the kettle. "Your Grandparents and Aunts have called as well of course; I've told them you don't have a phone at the minute but you're safe and well and just to give you a few days." I could tell mum was trying to be nonchalant. Like her only daughter wasn't splashed all over the news and there weren't stitches in her forehead.

"Mum, you've got to know…" I started and she paused almost instantly, looking at me encouragingly. "It was scary, and horrible, and I wish I could explain to you exactly what happened but I…" My voice caught in my throat. I couldn't re-live it all. So much had happened since Friday night and I needed to get that straight in my head. She sat down next to me and placed a reassuring hand on my arm.

"It's ok Emily, when you're ready to talk about it, I'm here and if you're never ready to talk about it, that's fine too. I can only begin to imagine what it was like, but I'm here for you. That's all you need to know." She smiled at me sympathetically. The urge to confess to her about the people I had been seeing, about the man in the trees with eyes that shone like honey, who made me tremble with fear and something else, maybe awe. I was prevented from any revelations when I heard the front door swing open and a tall, lean woman with dark skin and curly afro hair came striding through into the kitchen like an Amazon.

"Emily," She cried, warrior like, as she scooped me up in her long arms.

Mum smiled as she watched our tangled embrace. "I'll leave you two to catch up," And she headed upstairs to give us some privacy.

"Dude I was so worried! We heard about what was happening while it was still happening, it was all over the news. Jack called me and told me to turn on the TV and I was like, I hate watching the news, and he told me to shut up and turn it on. Then I realised it was at a theatre in London and I couldn't remember which theatre you said you had started at so I had to search through my texts and you should have seen my face when I realised. Christ I've never been so scared. I kept calling you and it kept going to answerphone and no one knew if anyone was dead or alive. Then the death count came in and it wasn't looking good, then I finally got a message back from your mum and she said she was sure you were alive, but they wouldn't let her see you. She made me promise not to come down to London and that I could see you as soon as you were back, but my God this has been the longest two nights of my life." She finished, detangling herself from me and grabbing the chair next to me. I smiled through her rambling and tried not to laugh. Only Nicki could make this dramatic experience all about her. She looked me up and down. "The stitches look neat; you shouldn't scar too badly." She stated, eyeing them curiously.

"That's what they tell me." I responded off-hand, wanting to duck down my head.

"Well, are you going to tell me?" She swatted at me playfully. "How did it all go down? How the heck did you survive it?" She looked at me earnestly, like she was asking me about how my last date went, rather than a terrorist attack. Annoyingly for me, she wasn't as patient and thoughtful as my mother, and more annoyingly, she wouldn't let it go without an answer.

"I played dead." I responded, all emotion gone from my face and voice. "I got lucky, that was all." I finished, hoping she wouldn't need more than that. I wasn't ready.

"Wow, you're one lucky sun of a gun that's for sure. Did you know you're all over the news? Everyone is asking about you, calling you some beacon of hope in this dark time. You know you could get a bundle of money doing some sort of interview for a big shot magazine right? Do you want me to be your agent? I'd be a kick ass agent." She grinned and it was difficult not to smile back. Nicki had always been the one to bring energy and light into the world, to see everything from a positive perspective and to make everything else not seem all that bad.

"No, I don't want to do anything like that. Re-living it all… it's hard to get it all straight in my head. Whatever I said in an interview, it might get mixed up, or said the wrong way. So many people died, I just wouldn't want to upset anyone by saying the wrong thing." I told her honestly, getting up from the table and taking my plate to the sink.

"Yeah I get it," She answered. "Maybe when it's not so raw… I think that the things you say could also help a lot of people, help them get some closure maybe." She said wisely. I hadn't really thought of it like that. All I could think of was the hundreds of family members waking up today without their daughters and sons or mothers and fathers and grandparents that still had so much life to live. And here I was, with a few stitches and the knowledge that life would never be the same.

I paused for a moment, listening to the footsteps of my mum upstairs, making sure she wasn't listening. "Look, I need to tell you something," I started, sitting back down at the table. "And I don't want you to tell me I'm crazy, because I already think that I might be. Or say that I've just been through some traumatic experience, because I know I have. But what I'm about to tell you is as real to me as those terrorists at the theatre. As real to me as you are sitting in front of me." Nicki raised an eyebrow as I took a deep breath and tried to blurt out the words before I changed my mind. To say the words that I hadn't even said to myself yet. "I think… I'm seeing dead people."

CHAPTER 6

I had expected Nicki to laugh, or at the very least ask me to repeat myself. But she looked at me with her large brown eyes and urged me to continue. "I can't get into it here, mums upstairs and she's concerned enough as it is." I told Nicki. I could deal with it if Nicki thought I was crazy, but I wouldn't be able to bear it if mum did.

"Ok," Nicki said slowly and nodded. "Let's go out and get some coffee, shops should be opening soon." She told me, glancing at the time on her phone.

"I can't go get coffee!" I said, incredulous, trying to keep my voice down. "My face is all over the news, by now they'll know my hometown, I'm surprised I haven't got journalists knocking at my door," I exclaimed, gesturing to the front of the house.

"Right, of course, sorry," she nodded again, and stood to pace the kitchen in contemplation. "Ok, we'll go for a walk in the park, plenty of space and time to talk properly." She suggested.

"No," I said quickly. "Not the park." I offered no explanation as I avoided her questioning gaze.

"Ok…" She said curiously. "My house?" She offered.

"It's a Sunday, won't your parents be home?" I asked, not wanting to risk being overheard and carted off to some kind of institution.

"Ah yeah, of course." Nicki said, smacking herself playfully on the forehead.

"Ok, alright, we'll do the coffeeshop, I'll just wear a hat and some sunglasses or something," I shrugged, running out of options. This wasn't a conversation that I wanted to get into in my tiny house with mum not far away, and now that I had said the words and wasn't greeted with mockery, I was eager to tell her more. If I could explain it to her, maybe it would make more sense to me, or maybe Nicki would have an explanation I hadn't thought of yet.

I popped upstairs to tell mum we were going into the shopping centre. She hesitated for only a moment, probably struggling with the fact that her daughter was an adult and she couldn't tell her not to go, and her desire to keep her home and safe. I grabbed a baseball cap I found stuffed into the back of my wardrobe and some overly large sunglasses. The baseball cap covered my stitches nicely, and only felt a dull throb from the material rubbing against them as I secured it on my head.

The shopping centre was only a ten-minute walk from my house, in the opposite direction of the park. I remembered the first time that Nicki and I had been allowed to walk to it alone, and wander around the shops idlily, looking at clothes we couldn't afford and basking in our new found freedom; our world had just become bigger. On the walk up, Nicki prattled on about her job, working in sales, which she hated but was just trying to save up enough to move somewhere exotic. We tried to discuss normal things, like dates that Nicki had been on and how her dad was driving her crazy. I barely heard a word as I tried to figure out the things I was about to tell her, and Nicki patiently rambled on, clutching at the most mundane things to talk about until I was ready.

The coffeeshop had not long opened when we got there, but there was already a smattering of people caressing their coffees and flickering through the morning paper or playing on their phones. We ordered our coffees with no queue to contend with and found cosy seats by the window.

I gingerly took off my sunglasses and tugged down my baseball cap a little lower.

"So… dead people?" Nicki asked softly, keeping her voice low. The gentle conversation from nearby tables covered our discussion nicely enough.

"After it all happened," I began, trying to skip over the worst part. "I had passed out and when I came to, everything was quiet, but there was this woman, standing over me, she told me to be still and that it would be over soon, but it wasn't safe yet. She stroked my arm and tried to reassure me, but I passed out again shortly afterwards. It was all very real. I felt her hand on me, I heard her voice. It was so real that later, at the police station, I asked for them to find her, sure that she had survived and managed to escape. They assured me that no one had escaped, that no one else had survived. That woman had probably been killed before I hit the floor. I recognised her though, I saw her in the mass of people who had run to the foyer. If she had died before I'd even passed out, how was it that she was there, next to me, talking to me?" I spilled all this out and then took a breath. Raising my eyes to meet Nicki's, I could see her watching me carefully, her expression blank. "I know what you're going to say, we took the same psychology lesson at A-Level. Maybe my brain was trying to reassure me, by creating a figment of imagination, of the last kind face I had seen before it happened, but I can tell you now, I *know* it was real. As real to me as you are now, I have never been the type of person to create these things in my mind, even when I dream, I always know it's a dream. I have never had the experience of 'did that really happen?'. I *know* that this happened." I finished defiantly. Nicki nodded and opened her mouth to speak. "There's more." I cut in and her mouth closed slowly. I told her about the little girl in the hospital, who was neither patient nor visitor and her disappearing crayons, then about the policeman at the station, who had disappeared before my eyes whilst the other police officers hadn't blinked and had looked at me like a crazy woman when I'd tried to thank the thin air. Everything that I had seen in the last day or so came spilling out of me in a wave of relief and fear. I took a slow sip of my coffee, which was now cold. I watched as Nicki lent back in her seat and let out a long breath. She ran her hand through her curly black hair and looked out of the window, mulling over the words she would say. "Do you think I'm crazy?" I asked in a small voice. Nicki flashed me a brilliant smile, the kind of smile that made boys flock to her and made girls trust her.

Nicki had always been the popular one, friendly, chatty and confident, she made friends wherever she went. She was fearless and strong, both mentally and physically. She had played every sport through school, primary and secondary and had no end of invites to parties and gatherings. And through every clique she was invited into, Nicki had never once faltered in being the best friend to me, her loyalty never wavering. "No, I don't think you're crazy," she answered through her brilliant smile. "I think you're fascinating." She declared, her eyes alight with curiosity and something like delight. "When I was travelling, I saw a lot of things, heard a lot of stories and experienced some things that I could never really explain." Her face grew more serious and I let out a breath that I hadn't realised I'd been holding. "I've never seen a ghost, but I think it would be naive of us to think that nothing happens after we die. That our energy and souls just disappear the minute our bodies stop working. All the things that make us who we are, must be so much more than just the blood and bone that we're made from. And a brush with death like yours... if that doesn't change you in some sort of way, then I don't know what will." She finished. Relief flooded through me, so glad that I had chosen to share this with her. No judgement or condemning, just understanding and acceptance. "The question is... what are you going to do with it?" She asked, leaning forward, our coffees abandoned.

The question threw me. "What do you mean?" I asked, my eyebrows creasing together.

"Well, if you are really seeing dead people... well, it's a gift that you don't want to take for granted. You could help people, maybe pass on messages to loved ones, help solve murders, you could even get famous for it if you really wanted to," she shrugged. "The possibilities are endless."

"I haven't thought about it, I guess." I responded. All this time I'd just been wondering what it all was and what it meant and if it were real. Not what I would do if it was true. "I can't tell anyone else; I can't be that crazy girl who survived a slaughter and now sees dead people. I can't be the girl who goes on stage and tells people I have a girl in red standing with me, beginning with the letter R. That's not me." I shook my head, dread passed through me at the mere thought of it. "Nicki, I don't want to see dead people. I just want it all to go away." I told her honestly. I leant back in the cosy chair and closed my eyes. Nicki leant across the table and took my hand in hers; it was cool in my clammy hand.

"Em, I don't know for sure if this is all real or not, or if it's here to stay. But if it is, you need to find a way to accept it and deal with it. It might be a part of your life now and if it is, you need to find a way that works for you." She rubbed the back of my hand sympathetically with her thumb. I gave her hand a squeeze and sat forward, looking into her earnest brown eyes. "I'll help you, if I can." She finished. Tears sprang to my eyes. It was nice to feel a little less alone.

"Thank you." I answered and let go of her hand. "Maybe it was all a fluke," I shrugged, saying it more confidently than I felt. "Maybe it's all gone away now. Maybe I just needed a good night's sleep?" I smiled and Nicki smiled back.

"So, you haven't seen anyone since last night?" She asked.

"Well there was this freaky guy in the woods this morning, but I think he was creepier than a ghost." I half joked; the stranger's amber eyes flashed in my mind.

"What guy?" Nicki asked, her eyebrows furrowed. I shrugged it off.

"Thinking back, I think he might have been a journalist," I pondered. "It's fine, I ran off like a crazy person." I told her, trying to shake the image of the man from my mind. I looked out the window again and watched as shoppers wandered past, going about their day without a care in the world.

"Yeah you're going to have to be more careful about that for a while I think," Nicki responded. "Or if you give one interview and that interviewer has full rights to your one and only interview, that might keep others at bay." She suggested, drumming her fingernails on her empty coffee mug.

"Maybe," I said, uncommitting. That was a whole other problem. We sat in silence for a moment as I watched the people out of the window. How many of them had watched the news? How many of them knew people that were in the theatre that night?

"We could do a Ouija board." Nicki blurted out suddenly as the thought came to her. "If we really want to see whether it's still happening, how real it is. My mum has one at home, we could summon someone forward, speak to them, maybe get some more understanding about it all." She reeled off excitedly.

The suggestion filled me with horror, the thought of willingly contacting someone dead, asking them questions. "I can't." I shook my head. "Nicki, I'm *scared*," I looked at her pleadingly. She might be fearless, but I wasn't. The one downfall of Nicki is that she couldn't always comprehend why people were scared of the things that she wasn't. She could walk into a room and command complete attention and authority and couldn't understand why others couldn't. 'Just decide to not be afraid' she would always say, as if it were that easy.

"Emily," she said sternly, looking deep into my eyes. "You can't always help what happens to you, bad stuff can happen, bad stuff *has* happened, and you have absolutely no control over that. But what you can control is how you deal with it, and how you let it affect you. You have complete control over your feelings and your actions. You can let this bad thing completely take over your life, and you can let yourself be scared and become a shaking wreck, rocking back and forth in a corner somewhere, or you can take control of it. You can decide to not let it take over your life, you can decide to not let it scare you. That is completely *your* decision and yours alone." She finished. I looked at her with a mixture of awe and fear. She was always a good one for inspirational speeches.

I didn't understand everything that was happening, I didn't understand why I had survived the terrorist attack when over a thousand people hadn't. And now people were disappearing in front of me and none of it seemed to make sense. I needed answers.

I hesitated for only a moment. "Ok, let's do it."

CHAPTER 7

When we got back to my house mum was sitting on the sofa eating lunch, she muted the TV as we entered.

"Hey you, I've just made some lunch if you want some?" Mum said getting up off the sofa.

"No, it's ok, we were thinking of going over to Nicki's to get some," I answered and Nicki gave one of her award winning smiles.

"Oh ok, no problem, I'll finish up and give you a lift." Mum said smiling back. Relief seemed evident on her face. Did I look happier? Maybe a little more normal? Having this weight of a secret off my chest certainly did make me feel better. But the anticipation of what we were about to do hung in my mind like unwanted fog.

"That would be great," I replied, trying to seem casual. Mum finished the last bites of her sandwich and grabbed her car keys.

"Shotgun!" Nicki called as she attempted to race me to the car, as if I could ever win.

"Cheater," I mocked her.

Nicki gasped, pretending to be insulted. "It's not cheating if God decided to grant me with incredibly long toned legs." She bragged, getting into the car. I rolled my eyes and poked a tongue at her. Mum laughed as she turned the key in the ignition.

Immediately the news started pouring in from the car radio. "... *Anderson was the one and only survivor in a terrorist attack that has gripped not only the nation, but the world...*" Mum switched it off as fast as she could. My good humour faded. The reality of what has happened and what was still happening sank in once again. It had only been two days, but it felt like it would never really go away. I would always be the girl that had survived by pretending she was already dead.

"So, did I tell you Jack lost his job?" Nicki asked, turning her head to me, attempting to change the subject. "For a ridiculous reason as well, I've told him he should sue. His boss keeps picking on this one girl, makes her do the crappy jobs that no one wants to do, belittles her and undermines her, it's awful. Jack had the guts to stick up for her and was handed his P45. I mean, I'm sure there's more to it, but it stinks, he really loved that job." Nicki complained.

Jack was a good friend of Nicki's, they had dated for a while back in school when they were younger, but they very quickly found out they made much better friends and had stayed close ever since. By association it made Jack and I friends as well. He was a good guy, fair haired and resembled someone who could be in a boy band, all sweetness and light. Nicki had suggested that him and I give it a go but I had no real want or need to be compared to Nicki in any aspect, knowing I'd always come up short. Dating me after dating Nicki would be like riding the merry-go-round after a roller coaster. "That sucks," I replied, realising I hadn't responded. Jack had always been the type of boy at school that would stop children from bullying each other. With his natural tall and stocky frame, no one dared question him, not that it ever resorted to violence, he had never been one for that.

Mum waved us off after she dropped us outside Nicki's house, Nicki insisting she would give me a ride back in her dad's car later. As we got inside, I was bundled up into the arms of a larger, older version of Nicki.

"Oh Emily, we were so worried." Mrs Williams swung me around similarly to how her daughter had earlier. I smiled and hugged her back fondly.

"Don't worry Mum, I'm fine," I said. I had called Nicki's mum 'Mum' since our second year in Primary school. It's what Nicki had called her so it's what I had called her too, and she had always seemed pleased with that.

"Em, why don't you head up to my room and I'll bring up some lunch?" Nicki suggested. I nodded as I untangled myself from her mother and headed up the stairs.

"Mum," I heard Nicki say in hushed tones as I went up the stairs. "Me and Em have some important stuff to discuss, so could we have some privacy please?" She asked. I cringed at the thought of her mum finding us.

I couldn't hear her response as I got to the top of the stairs and headed towards Nicki's bedroom. Nicki's house was huge, especially compared to mine. With three stories, a balcony overlooking the vast garden and a TV in her kitchen and bathroom, it had been an amazing house for sleepovers and make-believe games. I had always been jealous of her house, but then it became part of my life as much as Nicki had. I got to Nicki's room and sat on her window seat as I studied her particularly messy room which was roughly the size of my lounge and kitchen combined.

"Got the board!" Nicki exclaimed as she entered the room and pushed the door closed behind her with her foot. She waved the Ouija board above her like a holy grail. My heart sank to my stomach.

"Are you sure about this?" I asked, letting the doubt show in my voice. Nicki's face fell.

"Em, I'm right here with you, and if we get to a point where you're really freaked out, we can stop." She suggested and reached for my hand to give it a squeeze. I attempted a brave smile but my mind was full of doubt.

Nicki kicked some clothes out of the way to make space on the floor and set out the Ouija board. "Do you know what you're doing?" I asked, peering over her shoulder.

"Yeah I watched mum doing it with a bunch of her friends a few years ago and we did it a few times while I was travelling. Was good fun, never got scary, just really cool." She responded placing the planchette, a wooden triangle with a hole in the middle, on the word 'goodbye' which peeped out through the hole. I decided they would probably have felt a lot different if they could see the ghosts instead of just receiving messages from them. "Ok, come sit," Nicki gestured to the spot next to her. "Ok, we both need to put two fingers on the planchette very lightly." She instructed. I did as I was told and watched as my hand trembled. This was a stupid idea, as much as I wanted to tell myself that I was not afraid, I *was* afraid. Afraid that some ghost was just going to materialise right in front of me and I was going to have a heart attack. At least before when it happened, I didn't know they were ghosts. What if someone appeared from the theatre? Angry and feeling unjust that they had died, and I hadn't? What do you even do with a ghost that's angry with you? Could you ever get away from it? There were so many things that I didn't know yet; I wasn't prepared. But it was too late. "If there are any spirits here present," Nicki began, my eyes jumped to hers in alarm. "Then please move to the word 'yes'." She finished, closing her eyes and taking a deep breath. I followed suit, closing my eyes seemed like a good idea right about now. After a moment I peeked open one eye and looked at the planchette. It hadn't moved. Nicki peeked an eye open too. "Maybe you should try it," She stage whispered to me. I swallowed a lump in my throat. This seemed like a really bad idea, but, like all through my life, I wanted to show Nicki that I wasn't a complete wimp. Like I was in control of this in some way. That I could be brave.

"If… erm… if anyone is there please let us know," I called out weakly, feeling pathetic. My voice did not have the same authority as Nicki's. She sighed heavily as again, nothing moved.

"It happened right away the last time," She muttered to herself. "Just give it a minute." She told me. "Do not be afraid," She called out into the room, louder now, and I cringed as I imagined her mother in the room below us wondering what in the world we were doing. "If there are any spirits here present, please let it be known. Use our energy and move the board to send us a message," She asked into the air. When the planchette still refused to move a flood of relief flowed through me. We gave it another moment then Nicki moved her hands off the board. "Well this was a bust," She sighed again. "I'm sorry," She told me, looking crestfallen.

"No, don't worry about it," I smiled, trying to hide my relief. "It was worth a shot." I shrugged, then felt a tingle behind me, like cold breath on the back of my neck, but so cold that it sent shivers down my spine. I froze, alarm bells ringing in my head.

"Don't be scared," I heard someone whisper behind me. I spun around quickly, flinging the board planchette across the room and making Nicki yelp in surprise. Getting onto my feet and backing away, I was greeted with an elderly woman, around 70 at a mild guess, with greying hair and a kind face. A face that resembled Nicki's.

"Grams?" I gasped, using the name that Nicki had always called her. Nicki's head whipped from me to the space I was looking at and back to me again.

"Em, that isn't funny," Nicki said quietly, struggling to gain her composure.

The older woman nodded. "I don't have long, my grip on this world won't last," She told me.

"What does that mean?" I asked, ignoring Nicki.

"What does what mean?" Nicki asked, confused.

"It means if you're looking for answers, I can't give them all to you. The dead don't belong in this world Emily." Grams told me, looking concerned. I tried to nod but instead shook my head.

"Did you hear us, on that?" I asked pointing in the direction of the Ouija board. Grams let out a gentle laugh.

"No silly girl, those things don't actually work. You can't speak to the dead through a chunk of wood." She almost rolled her eyes and I smothered a laugh. I was having a conversation with a woman who had died many years ago. My best friends Grandmother of all people. Then I remembered Nicki and turned to her quickly.

"Your Grams is here Nik," I told her gently. For once in her life, Nicki was speechless, she opened and closed her mouth like she was impersonating a goldfish.

"It's not a joke." Nicki stated, as if talking to herself and looked over towards the space I was talking to.

"It's not a joke." I repeated as I shook my head, surprised that I wasn't afraid anymore. What was there to be afraid of? This woman had baked us cookies when we were growing up, had given us pocket money to buy sweets and convinced Nicki's mum to let us have the TV in Nicki's bedroom during sleepovers.

"Emily, I came to warn you, you need to be careful," Grams hushed tones brought back a sense of fear. "I didn't come for you, but I sensed that you were here. I could feel your warmth and your glow. Everything is grey over here, but you – you're swimming in light." She said, almost in awe. "If I can feel it, so can others." Her thick Caribbean accent was so real to me, she seemed so alive.

"What is she *saying*?" Nicki asked as I stared into her room, at a seemingly empty space.

"She's warning me, ghosts can sense me," I stated in an emotionless voice. "What does that mean Grams? Will they follow me?" I asked. My memory of the man in the woods sprang to the front of my mind. Hadn't he said something along those lines? That I was glowing? That he had followed me? Had he been dead? I swallowed my fear to search Grams eyes that mirrored the concern and fear that I felt.

"The dead don't follow the living," She informed me. "We visit, but not for long."

"How do I get them to stop? Why am I seeing them? How do I *stop* seeing them?" I asked desperately. The one question that I really wanted to know.

Grams shook her head. "You have a gift Emily, I don't know why or how, but you have. This isn't a gift that can be given or taken away." She answered, my heart dropped to my stomach. I nodded slowly. She reached out to gently stroke my cheek as an unexpected tear rolled down it. Instead of touching me, her hand went straight through and a shiver of cold went through me.

"I can't feel you." I stated, looking confused.

She shook her head. "My grip on this world is not strong." She repeated and looked behind her, as if someone was calling for her. "It's time for me to go. I will try to check up on you." She answered, her eyes lowered to Nicki. "Tell that one I'm proud of her. And tell her… that she and I both know where her heart lies. And it's not here." She finished. I nodded, looking at Nicki and her confused face while she patiently waited for me to stop talking to myself.

"Thank you," I whispered, the words sticking in my throat.

"Be careful," She warned again, she seemed to shimmer in front of me, almost fading. "There is darkness here and others have a stronger grip on this world than I," She told me, her grey hair and dark skin fading slowly. I went to ask another question, but she was gone.

CHAPTER 8

I relayed the conversation back to Nicki once I was sure Grams was gone. She welled up when I told her that her Grams was proud of her.

"She always wanted me to go out and be free – She got married young, had a bunch of kids and was a stay-at-home mum all her life. She knew I was never about that life." Nicki sniffed. She stood in contemplation for a moment and turned to me. "This is wild Em, you did it, you actually did it!" As if she had only just realised what had happened.

"I know," I shook my head and smiled. "I see dead people," I quoted from the film and we both laughed nervously. "I can't ignore what she said though. This isn't going to always be nice old ladies passing fond messages onto their grandchildren." I observed and Nicki sobered up.

"Yes, you're right. We need to find someone who knows about this kind of stuff, who knows how to deal with it." She looked at me. I looked back, helpless.

"Do you *know* anyone like that?" I asked her. She looked as helpless and as lost as me.

"No," She shook her head. "There are famous spiritualists and things out there… but how do you know if they're telling the truth or not?" She pondered.

"Never mind that," I dismissed her. "We'd need to find out how to actually contact them first." I remembered doing a report at school for a business class and sitting down with my mum and interviewing her, she was nicknamed a 'marketing guru' at work and offered me an insight into my project that even Google couldn't present. I needed my own 'ghost guru'.

"I guess we could Google it?" Nicki said, almost reading my mind. "Look up ghost experts or spiritualists in the area?" She got up to find her laptop. I nodded in agreement.

"It's worth a shot, there are loads about, I'm always seeing posts on Facebook of people looking for mediums and whatnot and people recommending them. There are probably loads out there, if I meet a bunch of them, at least one of them has got to be for real." I hoped but didn't feel confident.

An hour later we had Googled until we could Google no more. We had put together a list of potential ghost gurus, along with their websites and e-mail addresses and contact numbers. Nicki printed off the list since I didn't have a phone for her to send it to.

"Ok that's enough work for the day." She declared as she tucked the printout into my bag.

"Yeah I'm exhausted," I told her truthfully. I had been quite proud of myself, how I'd taken it in my stride with minimal freak out, but the whole situation had drained me. "Let's eat!" I demanded, my empty stomach grumbling.

We spent the rest of the day talking with Nicki's parents, eating and laughing and talking about the things we used to get up to when we were younger. Nicki carefully skirted away from topics and stories that might involve her Grams and I blissfully joked and laughed about things that had nothing to do with terrorists or ghosts. It made a nice change of pace.

After Nicki had dropped me back at home, mum told me that she had ordered me a new phone and that it would be delivered in a couple of days, I thanked her and we curled up on the sofa and watched the kind of Disney films we watched when I was young. Part way through The Little Mermaid I started crying. It began with a few delicate tears and then developed in massive, heart wrenching sobs. Mum said nothing and I said nothing, she just held me as I got it all out and she stroked my hair until I fell asleep.

In the morning, I woke, still curled up on the corner sofa, by sounds of breakfast being made in the kitchen. Last night's tears had dried on my face, making it feel tight and stiff. I stretched out as I tried to remember a dream I'd had. All I could remember was running... or maybe that was all I wanted to remember.

"Don't open the curtains!" Mum called from the kitchen as she heard me get up. I shot a quizzical look at the curtains, as if expecting them to set on fire.

"...And why not?" I asked, rubbing my eyes as they adjusted to the light of the kitchen.

"The journalists have figured out you're not staying at your flat. They're outside the house." She stated matter-of-factly as she turned the bacon on the grill. My heart sank. Slowly I moved back into the lounge and lined my back against the front wall and moved the curtains aside ever so slowly to peek through. There were roughly a dozen people camping on my front garden.

"Great," I muttered. Wasn't there some sort of law where I had a period of mourning or something?

"I've taken a few days off work," Mum told me as I went back into the kitchen. "We'll just wait them out. They'll give up eventually." She hoped, not sounding convinced.

"So, we just sit at home all day and night and wait for them to go away?" I asked. To be honest, it didn't sound like the worst thing, but I had my list of potential ghost gurus that I wanted to visit, how could I know if they were legit from just a phone call? It was something I wanted to sort sooner rather than later. A task I had set myself to keep my mind from darker thoughts.

"Do you have a better idea?" Mum asked me, looking at me pointedly. I knew what she was asking, if I just spoke to them, they'd go away. But this wasn't some celebrity gossip, this was so much bigger than that. World changing, even. One wrong word and it would be all over the news in minutes, it would change my future even more than it had already done. The world could end up hating me or loving me, and all I wanted was to be forgotten about; to go back to my life in London. Eating take-out food at a different place every night after getting paid, then bulk buying pasta and sauce and managing on that for the rest of the month. Back to binge watching Netflix series and complaining that I was too tried for work. Catching the sweaty tube and trying different methods to make my commute 30 seconds shorter. I wanted to get lost in a crowd and no one know my face. Instead, here I was hiding at my childhood home from journalists, eating bacon sandwiches and deciding not to tell my mother I could see ghosts. I almost laughed out loud at the thought of it.

"We'll stay at home and wait them out," I confirmed, grabbing a sandwich.

The rest of the day passed with no dramas. I managed to get in touch with my boss at the theatre, who had gushed down the phone at how brave I was and when the theatre was back up and running my job would be waiting whenever I wanted to come back – *If* I wanted to come back. I couldn't risk calling any ghost gurus with my mum around, especially on her phone, so I'd have to wait until mine arrived for that. I focussed on idle chatter with my mum, mostly discussing what she had been up to recently, and how work was going at her agency. Sometimes the chatter would die down and there would be a gap on the tv between episodes and the room would be filled with silence. For a moment my mind would be filled with the deafening silence of the theatre, as the squeaky footsteps of terror faded away, which meant the only person I was left in the foyer with, was death.

*

The next day came and went as I patiently waited for my phone to be delivered, ignoring the dreams of horror that I was slowly becoming used to waking up from. Mum shouted down to me from the top of the stairs. "I'm about to have a bath but the online tracking says the phone has been delivered. I told them to put it round the back." She called. I got up off the sofa excitedly at the thought of a new distraction and went through the kitchen to the back door. I scanned the back step looking for a small brown parcel.

"Looking for this?" A smooth voice asked as I stepped out further in search of my package, which the stranger was holding. Eyes still shining like honey, the man from the park lounged casually against the garden's high fence, turning the brown box around in his hands, as if inspecting it. What was he *doing* here? I regarded him warily, my fight or flight reflex kicking in. "You know, you are surprisingly difficult to get alone," He told me, a smile played on his lips.

"And yet you seem to manage it," I replied sharply. My desire to run and my curiosity battled it out internally.

"Some things are worth waiting for," He replied and cocked his head as his eyes travelled over me, hungrily searching every part of me, as if committing it to memory.

Feeling safe with the door within arm's reach, I decided to bite. "Why are you here?" I asked, practically demanded.

He paused as he set the parcel down on the patio table. "I wanted to avoid the rabble at the front," He responded, nodding towards the front of my house. "I saw someone sneak around the back and wanted to make sure no one was trying to get in. They left this behind." He finished, gesturing to the parcel. He seemed so casual and so unfazed. As if wondering into a stranger's garden was no big deal for him, as if it could be something he did every day.

"It's just a phone," I answered, as if I needed to tell him anything.

He nodded but no emotion showed on his face. He hadn't really cared what was in the parcel it seemed.

I tried to study him without being noticed, but his eyes seemed to burn into me, I could feel his gaze on me, penetrating my skin. How could I have ever thought he might be a ghost? "You told me before, that you followed me and that I was… glowing, or something," I faltered, embarrassed, but needing to know what exactly he had meant by the words. "Why did you say that? Why did you follow me and what exactly is it that you want?" I probed, wanting a real answer. A proper answer that would make the butterflies in my stomach disappear and stop my fight or flight reflex from wanting to pounce. I turned my eyes upwards to meet his gaze, wanting to seem as unfazed as him at this unusual exchange.

"It is something my father used to say, when someone was full of energy, that they had an aura about them, that they just had *something* about them. He would say that they were glowing. If you spent your whole life wondering what that meant and what it was like to see someone glow like that, maybe you would follow it too, if you saw it." He answered, emotion was raw on his face now, a burning intensity that made me look away.

"So, you saw a girl you liked and followed her up the country?" I scoffed, trying to hide my embarrassment.

"Not just any girl." He stated firmly, his eyes flickered to my forehead.

I shook my head gently. "I'm nothing special," I disagreed and resisted the urge to bow my head. "And being stalked is not attractive." I added in quickly, ashamed that actually, I was kind of flattered. I squashed the thought down, thinking of how horrified Nicki would be if she knew I thought that. She would have physically kicked this guy to the curb after the second sentence. "You're not a journalist then?" I asked, leaning back against the door, feigning nonchalance.

He shook his head, but the corner of his mouth quirked up in a smile. "No, not a journalist." He confirmed, still keeping his distance.

"Then who are you exactly?" I asked, raising one eyebrow.

"You can call me Christian," He introduced himself casually.

"Christian," I repeated, enjoying the feeling of his name on my lips. It suited him. "I'm Emily," I told him.

"I know," He replied and my eyes flashed concern. "There is probably not one person in this country that does not know your face at the moment," He replied to my concerned expression. Something wasn't right here. Who follows a girl they've spotted in a crowd, up the motorway, follows her to the park to talk to her and then hangs out in her back garden waiting to talk to her? It bordered on psychopathic, regardless of how good looking they were.

"Well it was nice meeting you *Christian*," I lied. "But I'm sorry, whatever wild fantasy you're playing out with yourself here, I'm not the girl for it. You might have noticed, but I've got a lot going on right now." I turned to go, deciding that whatever was going on here, it wasn't the kind of distraction that I was looking for.

"I am not here to be a bother to you Emily," He replied curtly, as if insulted.

"You're not a bother," I answered sternly, my back still facing him. "Those people on my doorstep, *they're* a bother, not being able to leave the house to buy bread, *that's* a bother, you are insignificant on the rank of issues in my life right now." I said harshly and walked into the kitchen, slamming the door behind me.

As I left, I thought I heard him say something like "… see what I can do about that," but I couldn't have been sure.

I wasn't sure whether to call the police, or to wait until after mum came back down and explain to her about my unwanted visitor. Was he really any worse than the journalists that were camped out on my front lawn? Could I even trust that he *wasn't* a journalist? After all, the nurse had told me herself that they had had journalists try to lie about being related to me so that they could get the first words that might come out of my mouth and broadcast them for the world to read.

I hadn't made up my mind what to do by the time mum was out of the bath, but before she came downstairs, I tweaked open the front curtains slightly. All the journalists were gone.

CHAPTER 9

Mum pulled open the curtains. "Huh, they must have got bored," She shrugged after I told her that the journalists were gone. "How's the new phone?" She asked, seemingly not curious about the fact that journalists had just disappeared all of sudden.

"Ohh, yeah sorry the journalists must have distracted me," I lied. "Can you grab it for me?" I asked innocently, trying to make out I was really into the film on the TV.

"Yeah ok," she answered, with only a fleeting look of confusion she went to the back door and slipped out to get the phone from the garden. I held my breath until she came back and she gently tossed me the parcel. It seemed to buzz with electricity from where Christian had held it.

We spent the next hour setting up the phone and calling customer services to see if they could transfer over my contacts remotely. Once it was done, I spent another hour texting people, letting them know I was fine and safe, and yes, I had been through a lot, but no I didn't want to talk about it. I had a further half an hour phone call from my grandparents who were gushing down the phone. It was hard for me to talk to them properly, they had so many questions that I wasn't ready to answer. A stab of guilt went through me as I thought of the grandchildren that had been victims that night, who would never get a chance to speak to their grandparents again. Mum saved me from any more telephone calls as she declared that dinner was ready. As I got up, a text from Nicki's friend Jack flashed up on my screen.

Heard you're back in the digital world, welcome back, hope you're ok.
I smiled at my phone, that was sweet of him. I bet Nicki got him

to ask after me.

Yes I'm fine, thank you for checking. I typed out and paused, unsure about how to keep the conversation going. *Sorry to hear about your job, have you found anything else yet?* I finished and sent it. A text came straight back.

Yeah it sucks, massive drama over nothing really. Let me know if you hear of any job openings in a zoo! Lol. I smiled at the phone. We'd never really text before, I guess my newfound fame was useful for something. After scrolling through a few more texts from acquaintances I decided that was enough phone time for the time being. Perhaps if I did speak to a journalist, people would stop asking me the same questions. I didn't want to go out there and speak like I was some beacon of hope though. I didn't want to rub it in that I had survived, when so many people were grieving.

The next day, after many reassurances that I would be fine, mum decided to go into work now that the journalists were gone, and I spent an abnormally long time in the garden, peering around to see if I could spot Christian. I should have been thankful that he wasn't still hanging around, but I couldn't help feeling a tiny dot of disappointment. When I realised that Christian wasn't going to make an appearance, I got out my list of ghost gurus and my phone and got to work. I dialled the number at the top of the list. A woman answered.

"Oh hi, I'm... Emma," I faltered, deciding last minute to give a fake name. Close enough to my own that I would still listen if I heard it. "Is this Mystic Christine?" I asked, quoting the name written down on the sheet of paper.

"Yes, that's right," She answered. "How can I help you?" She asked.

"It's a bit of a long story but I wondered whether you could help me? I think I have the gift of 'The Sight' as well," I said using the words she had used on her website. "And I was wondering if you did any sort of mentoring as I could really use some help with this." I finished, damning my voice for shaking.

"Oh, I'm sorry, I'm afraid I don't do anything like that," She responded and promptly hung up the phone.

The next six phone calls went down a similar path. Whether they were afraid of being found a fraud or whether they didn't want the competition, no one seemed willing to help.

On the eighth call, I struck some luck. "I'm afraid I don't do one to one mentoring; however, I do host a spiritualist group that meets twice a month, we always love to see new faces," a mixture of excitement and dread grew in my stomach.

"What happens in the group exactly?" I asked, imaging a group of dark hooded figures, holding hands and chanting.

"Different things at every meeting, we start with meditation, to get into a good, relaxed place so that we can reach out to the spirits. Different people receive different messages, some are touched or spoken to, it can get very real but it's a safe space to practice." She informed me. It sounded terrifying, but probably no more terrifying than Nicki's Ouija board experiment.

"Can I bring a friend?" I asked, thinking of how Nicki's support and energy might be the only way I'd get through it without a complete meltdown.

"Yes, that's not a problem, as long as you come with an open mind and you have the utmost respect for our spiritualists and the spirits themselves." She responded warily.

"Yes, of course," I answered quickly. I wrote down the details, their next meeting was this Thursday. The sooner the better. I thanked her and hung up. Thank goodness I had a lead – and a room of potential spiritualists no less!

"I could come with you," A smooth voice called over. Once again Christian appeared as if from nowhere, leaning up against my fence, the very picture of nonchalance.

I jumped. Delight and disgust battled out on my face. "It's rude to listen in," I scolded him, folding my page of names and numbers in two so it couldn't be read.

"Then perhaps you should have stayed inside if you wanted privacy," He suggested and smiled at me as I tried not to melt, struggling to keep a stern look on my face.

"I thought you would have left by now; can't you take a hint?" I asked daringly.

"I thought I would give you the chance to thank me," He said. My eyebrows furrowed.

"*Thank* you?" I asked, disbelieving. He had some nerve.

"Do you think those journalists left of their own accord?" He asked, raising an eyebrow. I paused. So, he *had* had something to do with it.

"So, I've traded twelve stalkers for just one. I suppose that's a little better." I retorted, not giving him the praise he was obviously after.

"I prefer to call it perseverance," The corner of his mouth quirked up in a smile, like he was making a joke.

"I call it creepy," I told him, trying to shake his casual demeanour.

He ignored the comment. "You know, if you *are* seeing spirits, then I could help you with that," He offered, taking a step towards me. My heart started beating faster, he had heard everything I had said.

"For one thing, that's none of your business, and for a second thing, it's for a project I'm doing. Ghosts aren't real." I sneered at him, clearly rattled by what he had said. He openly laughed at the comment. Head back, roaring laugher that seemed to rip free from his throat, it was deep and heartfelt and brought an automatic smile to my face to watch. "I'm guessing you believe in ghosts then?" I asked. He shook his head, still smiling.

"Depends. Ghouls in sheets, trailing through the house wailing? No, I would like to believe there is something better for us in store after death." He took another step towards me and I could see how white his teeth were. I got up out of my chair, I wasn't sure whether I wanted to walk towards him or walk away, but I felt safer on my feet.

"What do you think happens then?" I asked curiously. He was only a couple of meters away from me now, the closest I had been to him.

He shrugged. "I am not in favour of the idea of Heaven and Hell, but I would like to think that we find some kind of peace. Eventually." He answered. Gently, he took another step towards me, as if I was a bird that would fly away if he got too close. Perhaps he wasn't wrong. "I think we spend our whole lives struggling, one miserable day after the next. We worry about how to pay our bills, what to wear, what to say. Will he like me, was she mean to me? Will I get the job I want, if I work harder will I get a promotion? We spend every day struggling with the same thoughts, just trying to make it to the next day, until finally, we make it to our last. Then what? We are doomed to watch others for eternity, following them around, watching them struggle? Seems a little unfair, does it not? I would like to believe after a lifetime of struggle, we are rewarded with peace. It is something that deep down, I think everyone wants." He finished, I stared at him sadly. Was he right? Was every day just a struggle? I remembered Grams and how she hadn't stayed around for long. Had she found peace?

"Maybe there is some sort of middle," I ventured. "A place for peace, but you can still check on your loved ones," I looked at him warily, a mere meter away from me now, if the wind shifted in the right direction I would be able to smell him.

"It is a nice idea," He responded. "The best of both worlds. Unfortunately, the stories we tell ourselves at night to make us unafraid of the waiting darkness, don't make it any easier when we discover it's not real." He mocked gently. He seemed to know more than he was letting on. His piercing amber eyes bore into mine as I tried to figure out if he was teasing me or whether he was genuinely interested in the conversation. I was forced to look away from his intense gaze, shyness sweeping over me.

"You said that you could help me?" I breathed, almost whispering now he was so close. "How can you help if you don't know what happens when we cross over?" I asked, my heart beating so loud that I swear that he could hear it.

His fingers reached over to tuck a loose strand of my hair behind my ear. "Because just because you're dead, doesn't mean you've crossed over," He whispered back as his fingers passed straight through my hair. A chill of cold went through me.

CHAPTER 10

"You're dead," I stated, not moving. I wasn't sure why, but I felt relieved. As if talking to some dead guy was so much better than having a live person stalk me and hang out in my garden.

"I thought I would ease you in slowly," He told me, taking a hesitant step back, looking less sure of himself now.

"You just look… so alive, to me." I said, staring at him, open mouthed. His whole being seemed to buzz with electricity, I could see every strand of his dark hair, which sometimes flopped down to cover half his forehead. I could see every fleck of his deep honey eyes and count every freckle on his nose.

"I am more alive than most spirits you will encounter." He answered. "Still think I won't be able to help you with your 'ghost problem'?" He asked, now smiling, nodding to the piece of paper I had folded and placed on the patio table.

"Why is it that you're more alive? How can you not touch me, but you touched my parcel? Did you first see me in London? Were you at the theatre?" All the questions came rushing at once, I bit down on my tongue to stop more from coming out. This was way better than a spiritualist group. I surprised myself by not being scared any longer. Christian wasn't some insane, volatile stalker. He was just like Grams.

"I can tell you everything you need to know, if you are happy to listen. I just do not want to give you too much too soon," He answered, his half smile played on his lips, as if happy to finally have my full attention.

"No don't worry," I said quickly. "I can take it, there is so much that I'm *dying* to know." I cringed at the expression I had used, but he didn't seem to notice. "Should we go inside?" I asked, nodding towards the door. My garden was big for a 2-bedroom house, which was the last house on a row of houses on a cul-de-sac. We weren't over-looked, and our only neighbour was an elderly man who rarely went outside. Privacy wise, it was pretty good, but some discussions should be kept indoors.

"I would rather not," He answered, looking warily at the back door. I raised an eyebrow curiously, a question for later perhaps. "I was near the theatre when it all happened, I saw the ambulances and police and I stayed nearby out of curiosity. I did not enter, however. With all the police and ambulances, I knew that death would be nearby, and there is not much worse than the newly dead." He told me, pulling a disgusted face.

"Why not?" I asked quickly, hungrily, desperate for knowledge.

His lip quirked up in that half smile thing he seemed to do when he found something amusing. "There is no tour guide to the afterlife, there is no one there to teach us how it is done and what comes next. We have to figure it out for ourselves. It is a confusing time and strangely enough, the newly dead are the most alive. Sometimes they do not even know that they are dead and being the one to tell them is not a fun job for anyone. Better that they figure it out on their own." He paused and looked sad for a moment, almost defeated. Like maybe he had tried and failed before at being the spirit guide that no one had. "They began to bring out the bodies. One by one. More ambulances had arrived, and they had to close down all the surrounding streets, it was getting bigger and bigger. Then they brought you out. You were unconscious but you were the most alive person I had ever seen. With this magnificent aura around you, I knew exactly what it meant. I knew what you were and what you had become." His eyes drifted to mine and then looked away quickly, as if it hurt to look at me for too long. I tried not to hold my breath as I listened. "So many people died that night, all at once, life had been taken so swiftly and effortlessly. All that energy, that lifeforce, just blinked out of existence. That kind of event leaves an imprint. A type of psychic energy that sinks into the ground. Usually you might find the ground absorbs that energy and it becomes a type of hot spot for paranormal activity. This time, I think instead of absorbing into the ground… I think it absorbed into *you*. It is where your energy comes from, giving you the power to have one foot in each world. I was not 100% sure, but I knew I had to find out. So, I followed you." He finished, his eyes drawing back to mine. I let out a long breath as I tried to absorb the information.

"Ok, so I absorbed hundreds of peoples life force so now I can see dead people." I said matter-of-factly, the sentence seemed even more absurd out loud than it had in my head. "So, you followed me to see if your theory was correct?" I asked him curiously. He laughed gently.

"Originally, I followed you for a theory, yes. Then I carried on following you so that I could have my first conversation with a living being in over 100 years. Then, after speaking to you, I suppose I could not help wanting more." He said and I dodged his gaze, a little embarrassed, and a little pleased.

"What did you mean when you said you were more alive than most ghosts?" I asked, remembering how he had fondled the phone package between his hands.

"We prefer the term 'spirits' – ghosts make us sound like something from a horror film," he laughed. "Unfortunately, what you said about having the best between both worlds, is impossible. There is this world or the other. At the beginning, you have a choice, you can cross over to the next world or you can stay here. If you have no one to explain that and you choose this world, you will never be able to move on, then it is easy to get trapped here, wanting to watch your loved ones grow old. The longer you stay here, the harder it is to cross over…the more real you can become here. There are some advantages… and some disadvantages." He faltered; the trace of a smile gone from his lips.

"What are the advantages?" I asked, partly curious, partly wanting the smile to return to his lips. He took a step back towards me.

"I can move and touch things, if I really want to, if I concentrate hard." He shrugged, he reached his hand up to my face and very lightly stroked my cheek. Nothing like the feeling of cold that had run through me when he had tried to touch my hair. Instead his touch left nothing but heat on my cheek. I gasped and automatically lifted my hand to my cheek. "You do not have to let this scare you Emily." He continued. "It could be something magical and amazing, if you let it." He whispered, as if worried that speaking too loudly might scare me away.

"It's strange, but the idea of seeing gh… *spirits* does scare me. But every time I've spoken to one, I've not been scared once." I told him honestly. It was no more different than speaking to a new person you've never met before. Perhaps I had watched one too many scary ghost movies.

"I could help you," He suggested. "The offer before was genuine. If you need a 'ghost guru' as you put it, I could do that. Help guide you through this other world." He looked at me expectantly, but I hesitated. It made sense, who better to teach me about spirits than a spirit himself? I couldn't help but wish I had Nicki's Grams instead. Someone I knew and could trust. Not that Christian *wasn't* trustworthy, but I didn't know anything about him. Other than he was dead, and really, that wasn't enough. But then what exactly would he gain from lying about any of it? What did he have to gain and what would I have to lose?

"Why don't you want to come into the house?" I asked, remembering the question I meant to ask.

"Ah," He began. "Now we come to the disadvantages. The more alive a spirit becomes, he gets certain… limitations. You have a strong connection to this house. It buzzes with energy and love. It becomes a sacred place and becomes a place very difficult to enter." He watched my confused expression and continued. "For instance, I was able to follow you into your flat in London easily enough. No strong connection there, too many different bodies coming and going, not calling it home for long, but I couldn't go into your friend's house, or yours." He finished, seemingly unfazed by his confession of how many places he had followed me to.

"You followed me to all those places?" I asked, surprised. "How is it that I've not seen you everywhere?" Confused, I lifted one eyebrow. I knew I should be scared, or at least annoyed, but mostly I was curious.

"Like this," He answered and disappeared in the blink of an eye. He didn't fade away like Grams had done, which made me wonder if she had done it for effect. After a moment he reappeared next to me. "I have to will myself to be here, in your world, just as I do when I want to touch something. It can be hard to explain but it is almost like being in three worlds. Four, for some spirits. For me there is your world, of the living, the Inbetween, where I am right now, seeing you and you seeing me, then the other world where I am alone. If two spirits want to see each other, they both need to be in the Inbetween. If two spirits were both in the other world, they would not see each other. It is like having your own world, where everything is grey and time moves faster. Nothing and no one to bother you. The Inbetween is more interesting, but the other world almost feels… less lonely." He explained.

"What about the fourth world?" I asked, wondering about Grams.

"I cannot tell you much about that I'm afraid. The fourth world is where you go when you cross over, where spirits go to… find peace. I assume." He sighed quietly.

"And you chose not to cross over?" I asked in a small voice.

"When I died, I left a lot of people behind that I loved. I wanted to look over them, look out for them. I did not know until it was too late that the longer I stayed here, the more impossible it was for me to cross over. By the time I was willing to give it a try, I was too late. My loved ones grew old and when they died, they did not have unfinished business, they crossed over without a second thought." He shrugged sadly, avoiding my gaze.

"Leaving you all alone," I stated. Automatically, I reached out to touch his arm sympathetically and shivered as I passed straight through him. What could it have been like, to spend years watching over your loved ones, waiting for them to die of old age so you could be reunited, only to find you couldn't cross over with them? Then spending the rest of your dead life all alone? Tears sprung to my eyes. There must be something I could do for him, some way that I would be able to help him, to get him to cross over somehow. Perhaps this is what I was meant to do, to help spirits cross over? Maybe that is why he followed me.

"There you are!" I heard mum call as the backdoor sprang open. I jumped and spun around guiltily. "What are you doing out here?" She asked. I grabbed my phone off the table, had the day really gone by that fast?

"Just making some calls, the reception is better out here," I lied easily, concerned at how easily and quickly lies could spill from my lips.

"Well come on in, I'm ordering a takeaway." She smiled. "Pizza, right? Your favourite?" She asked, beckoning me in.

"Right," I answered and followed her in, I glanced over my shoulder as I shut the door, but Christian was gone.

CHAPTER 11

The next day Nicki came over after I'd text her, telling her about the spiritualist group I wanted to attend.

"Could I invite Jack?" She asked, sitting cross-legged on my sofa. I shook my head.

"Ideally I would like to keep the number of people that know about this to a minimum. And when I say minimum, I mean just you." I answered. "At least for now, while I'm still figuring things out." For some reason, I had decided not to tell Nicki about Christian. What he shared seemed private and if I really wanted him to be my ghost guru, then I needed to show him that he could trust me. I would hold back on discussing him until I had his permission at least. He hadn't been out in the garden the five times I went to check on him that day, but I knew he wouldn't be far. Or at least, I hoped. There was still so much that we needed to talk about.

"Yeah I get it, he's just been asking about you a lot recently, thought it would be a good chance to hang out," She said and gave me a wink.

I rolled my eyes. "Ohh, yes, come on over Jack and watch me speak to dead people. Oh, and by the way, do you fancy a drink somewhere dark where no one will recognize me because my face is all over the news and I don't want to be swamped with journalists?" I said sarcastically. Nicki laughed.

"Ok, ok, I get your point. Speaking of which, what about if people recognise you at the group tonight? Won't that raise some questions or send a looney straight to the papers?" Nicki questioned.

"Wayyyy ahead of you." I smiled, ignoring the 'looney' comment. "I'm going to let you do something that you've been trying to do for years," I smiled at her confused face. "I'm going to let you do my makeup." Nicki jumped off the sofa.

"Yasssssss!" She yelled, throwing her arms into the air and I laughed openly. Nicki had tried for years to convince me to let her do my makeup. For the first few years it was just because she loved makeup and wanted someone to experiment on, then she was convinced wearing makeup would make me feel more confident – but every time I had let her try, I would make her stop before she even got started, seeing myself in the mirror and looking like a child trying on their mum's makeup for the first time. I had felt ridiculous. Due to my constant lack of makeup, any photos that had been dug up and splashed on the news, I had been bare faced, and as Nicki always said, makeup can make you into a completely different person, and I was hoping to bet on that tonight.

I went into my mum's bedroom, grabbed every piece of makeup I could find and let Nicki get to work. It was quite useful being a smaller version of your mum, sharing makeup and clothes would be a huge benefit – if I had any interest in makeup or her clothes, which I did not. After twenty minutes of makeup I sighed loudly.

"Is this going to take much longer? I want to finish and go before mum gets home from work, I don't want to have to answer a lot of questions." Nicki rolled her eyes at me.

"You're nineteen, not twelve, you don't have to answer anything that you don't want to."

I fidgeted in my seat. "I'm already lying to her about a huge thing, I want to try and minimise that as much as possible." I sulked.

"Stop moving, I'm almost done," She demanded crossly and held my face still with one hand as she finished another layer of mascara. "Ok, done!" She declared at last and held a mirror out for me to see.

I still looked ridiculous. Makeup just didn't suit me. All traces of my freckles had disappeared under a layer of foundation and powder. My lashes were about 3 times their usual size and my eyes were dark like a racoon, but also looked 3 times the size. I studied myself for a moment, not wanting to criticise Nicki, who looked very proud. Objectively, I suppose I did look different and the layer of makeup had almost made my stitches disappear. Almost.

"Thanks," I smiled at Nicki and decided that it would be fine, maybe a little too made up for a spirit group, but these people didn't know me, maybe I was always this heavily made up. I glanced at the time on my phone. "We'd better go." We grabbed our bags, turned off the lights and headed out the door. Nicki had convinced her Dad to let her have the car for the night. He kept offering to help buy a little run around of her own but she refused for the same reason she had refused to get her own place. She wouldn't be staying here long and didn't want any ties to Birmingham that would give her a reason to stay. I dreaded the day that she would leave again, leaving me in this mess by myself, but I would never be the person to ask her to stay.

The spirit group was held in a community centre only twenty minutes away near the centre of Birmingham. Luckily getting into the city centre was easy as it was the same time that everyone else was trying to get out. We got there ten minutes early and sat in the car.

"Can we go in now?" Nicki pleaded. "I *really* need a wee," She said, jiggling her legs in the driver's seat.

"No one is here yet," I said pointing to the empty car park. "And I don't want to be the first in and have to make weird small talk." I complained. I wasn't great at meeting new people, and small talk was the worst.

Nicki sighed and tapped her long fingernails on the steering wheels. "Sod it, I'm going in," She said and opened the car door. "If someone is there, I'll have a wee, tell them I forgot my bag in the car, then come back to you." She assured me before she slammed the door shut. I watched as she approached the community centre and tried the door. It opened easily, letting out a stream of light from inside.

"So, this looks like fun," a voice came from behind me.

"Holy shit!" I cried out as I jumped out of my skin and turned around. "Christian!" I scolded as I placed a hand on my dramatically beating heart. He laughed.

"I am sorry, but I was worried I would not get a chance to speak to you before you went in." He smiled, relaxed, like popping up behind me unexpectedly was no big deal.

"Well I did look for you today to ask whether you were going to come tonight," I grumbled, annoyed that I hadn't had any proper time to talk to him.

"You did?" He asked, looking pleasantly surprised. I shrugged and tried to look disinterested. "Ok, well I am sorry about that, but if you ever do need me, just call my name, I promise I will come running." He apologised. I wanted to ask him what he had been doing today, but it was silly to think he would actually just be sitting in my garden waiting for when I would want to talk to him again. He wasn't a pet.

"Look, I appreciate you coming, but I've got Nicki with me and I haven't really told her about you yet and I can't be having conversations to thin air," I cringed, hoping I wasn't offending him.

"Not a problem, I will not talk when she is around, or will not expect you to answer at least. I will be quiet and keep in the corner, you will not even know that I am there," He insisted. I nodded.

"Have you ever been to anything like this?" I asked.

He shook his head. "The thought of reaching out to the dead was only just introduced when my loved ones were around. By the time it gained popularity, I had no one I was interested in contacting." He shrugged.

"If those people in there really can contact spirits, they'll see you, won't they? What do you want to do about that?" I asked, panicking, I really hadn't thought this through.

Christian's lip quirked up in a bemused smile. "Emily, in all my years of wandering this earth as a spirit, you are the very first and only person I have come across who has been able to see me, I very much doubt that anyone in there can," He shrugged, then saw my concerned expression and sighed. "Fine, I might be better off stepping into the other world anyway. If another spirit does come through and wants to contact someone in that room, then I might scare them off."

"Right ok, good idea," I said. "I'm sorry," I quickly apologised. "I know that you want to help, but I've got to see what this group is really like, whether it could actually help me and-" I got cut off as Nicki opened the car door.

"You ok?" She asked. I nodded and my eyes flicked to Christian's, who rolled his eyes and disappeared.

"Yup, fine," I answered.

"You want to head in?" She asked, gesturing to the carpark which had begun to fill up without me noticing.

"Yes, great idea," I said and grabbed my bag and slipped out of the car, desperately forcing myself not to look in the back seat to make sure he hadn't reappeared.

We entered the community centre, just us two and walked through the foyer where the toilets were, through two big brown doors which held a large room with a dozen chairs in the middle, facing each other in a circle.

"Hi there, I'm Frankie," A woman smiled at us as they walked in, holding out her hand to shake.

"Hi, I'm Emma," I responded easily, taking her hand, using the fake name I had given on the phone.

"And I'm Grace," Nicki lied, holding out her hand to shake.

"It's lovely to see new faces, I think I spoke to you on the phone, Emma?" Frankie asked, turning to face me.

"Yes, that's right," I smiled, hoping to God that my makeup was enough of a disguise, she didn't seem suspicious in any way. "We're both very curious about spirits and hoping to meet like-minded people." I said, almost quoting off her website. She smiled warmly.

"That's wonderful, please, go take a seat, we have tea, coffee and biscuits on the table over there, please feel free to help yourselves." She told us, gesturing to the table on one side of the hall.

We nodded, thanked her and made our way to the circle of chairs. "What's with the fake name?" I stage whispered to Nicki.

"What, you get to do it and I don't?" She said in mock disappointment. "Why should you get all the fun?" She grinned, knowing full well that none of this was fun for me.

My eyes darted around the room as we took our seats, a few people were already sitting, chatting with others or eyeing us curiously, a couple more were making tea and three more came through the door. That made eleven in total, and no Christian that could be seen. Which was something, though it was nice to know that he was there, somewhere, watching.

After a few more minutes, Frankie called across the room "Ok ladies and gents, if you could all take a seat." And came across to sit with us. There was in fact, only one man in the circle with us, probably fifty or sixty years old. Actually, all the people in the circle looked roughly middle aged. Nicki and I stuck out like a sore thumb. Then a thought hit me, any of these people could be dead. I grabbed Nicki's arm quickly and whispered. "How many people are there?" I asked. She looked at me quizzically but eyed the circle of people, who were all now sitting.

"nine," She whispered back, "eleven including us," she said quickly, watching the panic rise on my face. I let out a long breath. Ok good, no one was dead. Yet.

"If you can all please welcome Emma and Grace who have joined us for their first time tonight," Frankie smiled, looking over at us. Everyone responded in quiet 'hellos' and nods and we nodded back and smiled. "First I'd like us to start off with a meditation, just to relax our mind and bodies for what we might experience tonight." Her words had the opposite effect on me. My body tightened as I realised something might happen tonight, and I was just opening myself up to it. There was still so much I didn't understand. As Frankie carried on, asking us to breathe deeply and keep our minds blank, I tried my best to concentrate on my breathing and the fact that I was totally safe. Not only was Nicki right next to me, but I also had Christian on the other side watching over me too. I was being protected from two different worlds for goodness sake, I was safer than I'd ever been. The thought didn't seem to help though. *Ghosts aren't scary*. I told myself. They're just like Grams and Christian, and the girl in the hospital and the policeman that had just watched. *I'm safe*. I insisted as I tried to pay attention to Frankie's words. I heard Nicki breathing deep next to me. *I'm safe, I'm safe, I'm safe.* My words didn't seem to be reassuring me and when everyone opened their eyes at Frankie's command, everyone looked calm and peaceful and I was fairly sure I looked like a nervous wreck.

"Tonight, we welcome you into this safe space," Frankie called out into the room. "Join us tonight, speak to us, touch us or send us a message." Frankie continued, holding her arms wide open, as if about to embrace someone in a hug. My eyes darted around the room in anticipation. "This is a safe space, and we'd like to invite any spirits present to join us. If you have any message for any of us, please let it be known. Or let your presence be known, by making a noise, or touching one of us." She called out, confident and clear. Smiling, anticipating faces peered out from the circle. Everyone hoping they would get a message or hear a noise or feel a touch. I held my breath.

"Oh, I feel cold, do you feel cold?" A woman with greying hair opposite me said.

"Yes, I feel it too." Said the woman next to her, who had her dark hair up in a bun. My eyes darted between them both, looking for a sign that someone was there.

"Did you hear that?" Someone asked and spun around in their chair to look behind them, we all followed suit.

"Can you see anything?" Nicki leaned over to me and whispered. I shook my head. Was it possible that a spirit could be doing these things from the other side, affecting us without being seen? Could Christian be doing it? Or was this simply suggestion and imagination? Wanting something so badly to happen that you think it is?

"Wonderful," Frankie called out. "Thank you for joining us spirit, please, continue to let yourself be known, come through as strong as you can now, so that we can all feel your presence."

We waited with our breath held, each one of us straining to hear something, see something.

"I can *feel* something," The woman next to me whispered in hushed tones. I didn't dare move to look at her. "It's something dark, I can feel it. There is no good intention here," She whispered, wide eyed and afraid. "He's come for you!" She suddenly shrieked, stepping back and pointing at me. Suddenly large puffs of black smoke seemed to be coming from the ground, rising quickly, above our ankles.

"Don't be alarmed," I heard Frankie say calmly, but I turned to Nicki who looked concerned. The smoke was rising quicker and quicker, up our legs but contained in the circle.

"Nicki," I said desperately, grabbing her arm but Nicki only shook her head, wide eyed and not knowing what to do or say. I tried to kick my feet out at the smoke but quickly realised I was rooted to the spot, unable to move. The smoke was paralysing me. As it crept upwards, it froze my torso and arms. I looked around wildly and everyone seemed to be staring at me. The smoke wasn't creeping up them, only *me*. Before the smoke reached my throat, I let out a final call. "Christian!" I called, loud and scared, then everything went black.

CHAPTER 12

I woke to Christian's large amber eyes hovering over me. I blinked trying to clear my head and my vision.

"She's ok," I heard Nicki say and Christian backed away as Nicki sat me up. "Are you ok?" She double checked as she looked me over.

"Yes I'm fine," I said quickly, looking from Nicki, to Christian, to the circle of people looking very concerned.

"Should I call someone?" Frankie asked Nicki.

"No, I'm fine," I repeated, using Nicki's arm to help me up. I looked at the chairs and floor, all traces of smoke gone. I looked back towards Christian, fear and questions in my eyes.

"I think I scared him away," Christian told me. "But we have to get out of here. *Now*." He insisted. I nodded curtly.

"I have to go," I said and looked on the floor for my bag. "I'm sorry, it was very nice meeting you all," I called over my shoulder as I headed for the door. As I left, I heard Nicki try to explain that I was a very sensitive person, and this happens a lot.

"What the hell was that Christian?" I asked as soon as the door closed behind me.

"I am so sorry," He said quickly. "If I thought there was even a chance that that could happen, I would never have allowed this," He insisted.

"That what could happen? That some smoke ghost could *paralyse* me?!" I almost screamed. "I thought I was *safe*, I thought all the spirits would be like you, or Grams or the others – what *was* that?" I stopped by the car and turned to face him. He looked tired and lost.

"That's what I would like to know," Nicki said from behind me. "What happened in there?" She asked. "And who are you *talking* to?"

"I think the smoke paralysed me and that's what made me fall, or black out." I shook my head. "Can we just get out of here? Now?" I asked nodding at the car. Nicki scrambled to find her car keys and Christian got in without the door needing to be opened. Strange that he could pass through the car door easily but not fall through the car seats. Another question for another day.

Nicki started up the car and pulled out of the carpark as quickly as she could. "What do you mean, black smoke?" She asked once we were a few minutes away from the community centre. I looked over at her.

"The black smoke in the circle of chairs," I stated flatly. What did she mean, what black smoke? Nicki shook her head.

"There was no black smoke?" She stated it like a question. I stopped to look at her for a moment. Had that really happened? Hadn't Christian seen it though?

"What exactly, from your point of view, happened in there?" I asked her slowly. Nicki shrugged as she signalled to turn right.

"We did the meditation and then Frankie called out for some spirits and then some people were saying they were getting cold, I asked you if you could see anything, you said no, then the woman next to you said she could feel something and looked at you, then Frankie told her to calm down and then you started kicking out your legs and then your arms and it was like you were having a fit. You called out for Christ and fell on the floor. Then you ran out. Really feel like I'm missing something here." She gave me a quick glance from the corner of her eye.

"So, you didn't see any smoke?" I asked.

"No smoke," She confirmed. I looked towards the rear-view mirror to see Christian's reaction but there was no reflection. I turned in my seat, but he was still sitting in the car. His eyes were closed, and his face was stern, as if he were concentrating on something. "Can you tell me what it is exactly that you saw?" Nicki asked quietly.

I paused, then decided to opt for the truth. "The woman next to me said she felt something… something dark. Then all this black smoke started rising from the floor, like something from below was on fire. But it was thick and really black and was about a foot thick on the floor before it started to wind itself up my body, paralysing me as it rose. I couldn't move, or at least, it didn't feel like I could. I called to Christian for help," I paused as Nicki's eyes flashed over to mine. "He's in the back seat at the moment." That time, both sets of eyes flashed towards me as I glanced over my shoulder. "Pull over for a sec," I asked and with a concerned expression, Nicki signalled and pulled over on a quiet side road. As I suspected, Christian's face relaxed as we came to a stop. "I'm guessing you have to concentrate to stay in the car while it's moving?" I asked him, my fear forgotten for a moment as curiosity took over. He gave a wry smile.

"It's a lot harder than it looks." He replied, relaxing in the seat for a moment.

"Ok, who the hell is Christian?" Nicki asked, seemingly annoyed.

"I'm sorry, I should have told you about him before, but it didn't seem like a good time and I wanted to talk to him again before I spoke to you about it and I just never got the chance." I explained quickly and pathetically. "Christian is the guy I met at the park," I continued.

"The journalist?" Nicki asked.

"The guy I thought might be a journalist. He's dead." I flashed Christian a look. "Sorry, he's a spirit." I corrected myself. Christian let out a small laugh. "I've seen him a couple of times since and he's helped me understand a little more about what I've been seeing. I hoped that maybe he could have helped us tonight. I mean, he did, but not in the way that I was expecting." I finished.

"Helped us how?" Nicki asked.

"Well at the end of the group, if nothing had come forward, I was going to get him to come in and see if anyone could see him and then I'd know if anyone in there had 'The Sight' or not. Doesn't matter anyway, he popped out of thin air to scare off the smoke ghost and no one blinked twice at him, so I'm guessing that answers my question." I sighed.

"He scared off the smoke ghost?" Nicki repeated, curiously. I looked over at Christian.

"I do not think he was expecting to see me. I did not see the smoke on the other side, otherwise I would have come to you sooner, it was only when you called my name and I came through to the Inbetween that I could see what was happening. Spirits can feel other spirits and I'm a lot stronger than him. It slithered away the moment I crossed over to you." Christian told me.

"But what exactly was it? How was that a spirit?" I asked, ignoring Nicki's question for now.

"It can get a little complicated, but like I told you before, there are different levels of how strong or how alive a spirit can be. That thing is barely alive, what we become in death can be a reflection on who we were when we were alive, and I dread to imagine what kind of life that thing had." He shook his head, a look of disgust on his face.

"Can it follow me?" I asked shortly. Christian's eyes gave away the answer.

"It knows that I am with you, it knows you are protected, I

highly doubt it would come back," He said confidently, but a little too quickly.

"I appreciate it, but I need to learn to protect myself." I told him. "Just in case, I can't always expect you to jump in for me." I sighed. There was still so much I needed to learn and figure out.

"Soooo…. Christian. Good guy or bad guy?" Nicki asked, interrupting us.

"Right sorry, he's a good guy, he's trying to help as best as he can from his side. Though he only knows the spirit side of things rather than my side of things, but it's still really useful," I added on quickly.

"Oh, so like your own ghost 'ghost guru'?" Nicki asked.

"We prefer the term 'Spirit'" Christian cut in.

"He prefers the term 'Spirit'" I replied once I remembered that Nicki couldn't hear him.

"Oh," Nicki replied. This was getting confusing. "Like a Spirit Guide!" She said suddenly.

Christian smiled. "I like that," He replied.

"He likes that," I answered for him and shook my head. "Look, it's hard enough keeping up with conversations with both of you, let alone interpreting a conversation between you both as well.

"Sorry, I just find it fascinating. There is a gh… Spirit in my car and you're just happily chatting away with him." Nicki laughed. "Man, this is awesome. Need to put you on TV," Nicki laughed again and went to put her keys back in the ignition. "Oh, serious question first. Is this smoke demon going to kill us all in our sleep or can we head back?" She asked lightly. I wasn't sure if she was mocking us or just trying to make light of the situation.

I half shrugged, exchanging a glance with Christian. "I think we're ok for now, but maybe we don't call out for spirits any time soon," I answered as Nicki started the car up and Christian went back into concentration mode.

I thought about the woman who had told us she'd felt something. I didn't remember seeing her when I woke up from the floor, but no one had freaked out that Christian had appeared. I was fairly certain that no one was able to see him. But then maybe there were different levels of abilities, maybe this woman couldn't see him, but she'd definitely felt the smoke spirit before it started happening, she had tried to warn me. It was definitely worth trying to get in touch with her again. Though I wasn't 100% convinced I'd be let back into another spirit group, not that I really wanted to. But perhaps there was another way.

As we pulled up outside my house, I said goodbye and thank you to Christian and he promised to stay on watch tonight outside the house, just in case. Bizarre that I felt safer having a ghost watching over me, but stranger things had happened this week. I called a 'hello' up the stairs to mum and heard a distant 'hello' back from the bathroom.

"If you hadn't just had a whack on the head from falling over, I'd totally be hitting you right now," Nicki told me as she closed the front door. I'd just explained that Christian couldn't get into the house.

"Why, what did I do?" I asked innocently.

"Er, duh, you met a guy that you like and didn't tell me!" She said in mock scolding.

"What, Christian? I do not *like* him," I said, appalled. "He's a ghost!" I exclaimed.

"Right, he's dead, so you need to stop blushing every time he looks and talks to you! Do you know how I knew when to shut up and let him talk just then? Because every time he speaks you go all doe-eyed and dreamy." She smiled but her eyes seemed cross.

"I do not!" I crossed my arms and furrowed my eyebrows. Nicki gave me her 'who are you kidding?' look. "Seriously! He's just helping me out, and it's nice to be able to talk to someone who kind of understands what's going on, but there is nothing more to it." I insisted.

"Uh-huh," She replied. "Tell me what he looks like," She asked, sitting on the arm of the sofa.

"Just, you know, totally normal." I replied, I could feel my cheeks blushing. God damn my body for giving me away, what a betrayal. Nicki rolled her eyes.

"Whatever you say. Look, I'm going to head off so you have a chance to wash your face off before your mum asks you why you look like a hooker, but seriously, you need to have a word with yourself. This is a brand-new world for you right now, and I get that it's scary and exciting and different, but you've got a lot more to figure out than how to talk to dead people. There are rules you've got to set out here and lines that you can't cross. Like don't get involved with the first hot dead person you see. Or any dead person for that matter. I love you Em, but you've always been guilty of falling for anyone who gives you attention. Don't let that happen here," She warned. She waved a goodbye and walked out the door.

She was being ridiculous. Yes, Christian was good looking, and he may have just saved her from some kind of creepy smoke spirit, and he might be giving her attention because she's the first live person he's seen for many years, but that didn't add up to what Nicki was thinking.

I grabbed the remote for the tv and turned it on absent-mindedly, sitting on the edge of the sofa.

How dare she tell me that I fall for anyone who gives me attention? That wasn't true… Was it? I mean, yes, it's always nice to get attention, especially from good-looking men. I mean, who wouldn't want that? But to basically accuse me of being an attention whore was a bit much. I gripped the remote tighter.

The thought of Christian's eyes staring above me, concerned, as I awoke, floated through my mind. His piercing gaze scanning me to make sure I was ok, that I wasn't hurt. His kind face relieved as I stood up and said I was fine, like he really, honestly cared.

I was stirred from my thoughts quickly as the remote control clattered on the floor below. I looked down, confused and looked back at my hands which were now clasped together, cupping thin air. How in the world could the remote have fallen through my intertwined fingers? My heart skipped a beat. I still felt the heat in my hands from holding the remote too tightly. The buttons still making a slight indent in my palm.

I was still staring at my hands when mum came down. "What in the world is that on your face?" She laughed and humiliated, I went upstairs to wash, all thoughts of the remote control forgotten.

CHAPTER 13

In the morning mum slammed a handful of post down on the breakfast bar and made me jump. "You've got fan mail," She told me as I started to leaf through the post. About a dozen letters, some handwritten, some not.

"Who in the world is writing to me?" I mumbled to myself as I opened the first letter. I scanned through it and then reached for another, tore that open and read that. Then another, and another. Mum turned around to watch me.

"Well?" She asked, curiosity getting the better of her.

"They're all from newspapers or trashy magazines wanting to interview me," I told her as I opened another letter. All offering different amounts of money, all differing in their plea to me, from a courteous suggestion to downright guilt tripping. Mum picked up one of the open letters and scanned it over.

"Wow, that's a lot of money," she stated with her eyebrows raised, she picked up another letter and her eyebrows got even higher.

"Yup, this is how much they offer to sell your soul," I scowled as I read the line *'it is your duty to the nation...'* on one of the letters. I could feel my mother's eyes on me, but she decided not to say anything more about it. I tried to swallow my anger, knowing full well that all these journalists wanted was to sell a story. They hadn't been there, hadn't experienced watching the horror on people's faces as they knew they were going to die. How people had tried to run, only to find that there was no way out. How could they possibly want me to talk about this? To regurgitate the experience for people's viewing pleasure? I could barely close my eyes without remembering the sea of bodies strewn across the floor. How could talking about it possibly make everything better?

"I've got to get to work, but are you going to be ok on your own for another day?" She asked, pouring coffee into a 'to go' mug.

"I'll manage," I replied with a wry smile, trying to shake the pensive thoughts from my head. She tapped her nails on her coffee mug and looked at me hard.

"I know I'm not great at the whole, emotion thing, but I am here for you. If you ever need me to take a day off or you need to talk, you just have to say the word. It's been really lovely having you around again you know," She smiled.

I smiled back. "I know mum, and it's fine, honestly. I just want to try and get back to normal as fast as possible. I'm not really sure what that normal is at the moment, so I appreciate you letting me hang around until I figure that out, but I know you're here." I got up off the stool and gave her a quick hug.

"Ok, enjoy your day. Try not to spend it all binge-watching Friends!" She called as she headed for the door.

As I finished my breakfast and shifted through the last few letters, my phone rang. Jack.

"Hi Jack," I smiled as I answered quickly, wiping crumbs away from my mouth.

"Hey there Emily! Long-time no speak, how are you doing?" He asked. I hated that question. How could I answer 'fine' when everyone knew I couldn't possibly be fine.

"Taking one day at a time," I answered, adding a small laugh on the end to make it seem less serious. "How about you?" I asked.

"I'm great actually, secured myself an interview at Twycross Zoo!" He told me excitedly.

"Oh wow that's amazing! It's a bit closer for you as well isn't it?" I asked.

"Yes, the pay is better too so I've got my fingers crossed." I could feel his smile through the phone.

"That's great, really pleased for you, I'll be sending good thoughts," I responded. There was a pause. Damn, how do I continue a conversation? Why was this so difficult? "Sooo... anything planned for this weekend?" I asked. Had he really called just to tell me he had an interview?

"Actually, that's what I wanted to talk to you about. I'm a big believer in positive thinking, so I've decided to act like I've already got the job so wondered if you wanted to go out to celebrate?" He asked. I paused for only a moment; celebrations were the last thing I wanted. Especially in a crowd of people where I wouldn't know who was dead or alive.

"Oh, er, maybe," I answered, not wanting to say no but not wanting to say yes either. "How many people are going to be there?" I asked cautiously.

"Oh," Jack laughed down the phone. "No, I meant, just you and me. Maybe dinner somewhere?"

"Oh!" It was my turn to say as I laughed a little embarrassed. Jack was asking me out for dinner. Me. For dinner. "Yes, ok, sounds good." I replied quickly before I could change my mind.

"Great," He sounded relieved. Had I made him nervous? "I'll pick you up around 7 tomorrow?" He asked.

"Looking forward to it," I replied, almost automatically. What was going on?

"Ok, bye for now," He said and hung up. I called Nicki almost right away. It only rung once before she answered.

"Did you tell Jack to ask me out?" I asked quickly.

"Whoa, morning to you too," She replied.

"Did you?" I asked again. If this was some kind of pity date because she thought I had a crush on a ghost, I would absolutely hate her. For at least a day.

"What? No, not at all! I did tell you he's been asking about you ever since you came back up this way." She answered.

"So ever since the incident last week?" I asked, wondering if it might be to do with getting a chance to talk to the only survivor of a huge terrorist attack, as no one else seemed to.

"Dude, I don't think it has anything to do with *that*," Nicki laughed. "He's always had a thing for you and by the time he got the courage to do anything about it, you went off to London. I think he's just trying to grab his chance while you're back up this way." Nicki said. "I've always told you that you two would be good together." She was right about that, but again I had always thought it was more to do with pity. Could I date someone that Nicki had dated? It didn't seem ethical, but she seemed more than happy with it. "So where is he taking you?" She asked curiously.

"Just out for dinner tomorrow to celebrate a potential job offering," I answered, calming down now that I knew it wasn't a pity date. Then my heart sped up. It wasn't a pity date. Jack liked me and wanted to go on a date with me. I was going on a date with Jack. Shit. What would I *wear*?

"Ah, the whole positive thinking thing ay? Sounds like a good plan." Nicki replied and I heard her filling up a cereal bowl through the phone.

"Nicki, I'm not prepared for a date. I didn't bring date clothes with me!" I sighed down the phone. It hadn't even crossed my mind when I was packing my suitcase.

"Ohhh, shopping trip?" Nicki asked.

"No," I answered. "I'm currently jobless and still having to pay my rent and bills." I told her. I had shifted my money worries to the bottom of the pile for the moment, but at some point, they would creep back up and would need to be dealt with.

"Ok, no problem, I'll come over tomorrow with a selection of clothes and we'll make something work," She offered.

"Ok great, you're the best," I answered, relieved. Nicki had more clothes than she knew what to do with, half of them still had the tags on and she had amazing taste in clothes, better than anything I had ever put together.

I hung up the phone and got myself dressed, thoughts of Jack and letters from the journalists still whirling around my mind. Hesitantly, I went to my back door. Would Christian be out there waiting? Would mum disapprove of me spending the day with an almost stranger who had pretty much saved my life who happened to be dead? Probably better than binge watching tv…

I took a step out the back door and waited a moment, when he didn't appear, I called softly. "Christian?" I asked. It was just a few seconds before he popped into view. "Hey," I smiled automatically.

"Hi," He smiled back and for a moment we just stood there, looking at each other.

"I didn't get a chance to thank you for last night," I told him, clutching at a reason to see him.

He shrugged. "That is what I am here for," He responded politely. "Something troubling you?" He asked, scanning my face. "There was no sign of last night's spirit here if that is what you are worried about?" He asked, taking a step towards me.

"Oh good," I smiled. "But no, it's not that, I've just had a bunch of letters from journalists wanting to talk to me." I shook my head. "I don't think there is any escaping this." I paused for a moment to look at him as he flicked his hair out of his eyes. Did his hair irritate his eyelashes when it fell like that? Could he feel it? I suppose there was no such thing as a spirit haircut.

"I am sorry, I suppose there is only so much I can do from this side." He sighed, running his hand through his hair subconsciously as he saw me looking at it. "I think if it is not going to go away, then it might be time to embrace it. But on your terms," He said, inspiration hitting him.

"What do you mean?" I asked. The sound of his voice was like an unheard song, I could listen to it forever.

"Well, you could decide to do the interview. You decide what questions get asked and what gets answered and how you answer it. You can demand final say on the edit, or do it live so no one can twist anything." He paused. "Have they offered you money?" He asked.

"Yes, some of them have, but I don't want it. I don't want people to think the only reason I'm coming forward now is for money," I put my hand to my temple and rubbed like I was getting a headache. The whole thing *was* a headache.

"No, but you could donate it? Get the journalists to bid against each other, highest offer gets the interview with all proceeds to be donated to the victims' families? To help with funeral costs and the like?" He suggested.

"Christian that's brilliant!" I exclaimed. "Why hadn't I thought of that before? That way I could get this all over with in one interview, the victims' families get something, and I don't have this hanging over me. Maybe even I could get some closure," I finished, finally feeling relieved. Maybe I could actually do some good. "Oh, Christian I could hug you!" I smiled and got lost in his huge honey eyes. He took a step towards me, smiled and held out his arms. I laughed nervously, but the serious look in his eyes made me stop. Still reaching out for me, I took a step towards him and before I knew it, I was lost in his arms. They felt strong and solid around me, my face nestled into his shoulder, I breathed him in but quickly realised he didn't smell of anything, but the warmth of him felt real. He *felt* real. If he hadn't spent last night invisible to Nicki then I would have sworn right then that he wasn't dead and that he was very much alive. As we let go of each other, I was lost for words.

"You hum with electricity you know," He told me. I raised my eyebrows.

"I do?" I asked nervously.

"Yes, I have never met anything as alive as you." He murmured.

"It's funny," I replied shyly. "Sometimes I think the same about you." I looked at the ground. We couldn't talk like this to each other. It wasn't right. He was basically a stranger. And dead. Don't forget, very dead. I went to sit at the patio table, trying not to meet his eyes. "I'm seeing a friend tomorrow night." I told him quickly. He turned to follow me to the table.

"Nicki?" He asked, resigning himself to the fact that the moment had gone.

"No, his name is Jack. We went to school together; I've not seen him for a long time. We're going out for dinner." I tried to shrug like it was no big deal, but the stilted sound of my words gave me away.

"Like a date?" He asked.

"I think so." I replied, still looking at the ground. He sounded tense.

"That sounds nice," He voice softened. "Where are you going?" He asked.

"I'm not sure, I'm hoping Italian, that's my favourite." I smiled, trying to appear more relaxed than I felt.

"Ahh, pasta and pizza. That always looked enjoyable." He sat on the chair opposite.

"You've never tried it?" I asked, thankful for the turn in conversation.

"No, it was more meat and vegetables when I was growing up." He laughed. "Food looks so much more appealing now, but then we did not have a problem with obesity back then either." He laughed again.

"Right of course, I keep forgetting that though you look in your 20's, you're technically much older." I smiled at him, reaching his gaze. "You actually seem quite modern to me."

"Ahh, I have spent years watching fashions come and go, trends fade in and out. I have watched the world adapting to a new era and I have done my best to adapt alongside it. There are a lot of experiences I cannot enjoy but there are some that I can take part in." He answered wistfully.

"Like what?" I asked, curious.

"Well, I cannot surf the internet, but I understand what it is used for and what it can do, and I cannot concentrate long enough to hold down a page of a book and read it in its entirety, but I can go to cinemas and enjoy all the Harry Potter movies." He smiled.

I laughed, he was a Harry Potter fan, amazing. "The books are better," I said automatically.

"That is what I have been told," He agreed and lifted his palms up in a 'what can I do about it' shrug. "But I have also had the delights of being able to learn almost every dance move through the last hundred years. You would be impressed with my Floss." He smiled. I looked at him open mouthed.

"You can do The Floss?" I laughed, thinking of the dance move me and my friends has been obsessed with a few years back. "Now this I have to see," My eyes went to his and lit up as he stood. He took a few steps in to the centre of the garden. Suddenly he straightened his arms and moved them side to side as he thrust his hip in the opposite direction. I almost fell off my chair with laughter. "That has to be the worse Floss I've ever seen," I laughed through breaths of air as I clutched my side. He stopped and grinned at me.

"Ok maybe it could use some work," He laughed and came back to sit with me.

"Ok, wait here, I have an idea." I told him as I got up off my chair and ran inside. I came back later with a book in my hand.

"What are you doing?" He asked, raising an eyebrow.

"We're going to read Harry Potter." I told him and opened it to the front page and moved my chair a little closer to him. I held the book open and began to read aloud. He shifted closer, a look of surprise and delight on his face. We spent the rest of the day sitting in the sun, reading Harry Potter and exchanging looks of anticipation as I read.

CHAPTER 14

"So, you've e-mailed all of them?" Nicki asked me the next day, as she spread clothes across my bed. I had just told her that I had decided to go ahead with an interview after Christian's suggestion.

"Yeah, them and some others that I found online. I lined out the questions I would be happy to answer and that I had final say of what goes to print or on air. I've told them highest bid gets it and all proceeds would go to the victim's families. There are already fundraisers online from what I've found so it should be easy enough, they can donate directly to one of them." I told her as I picked up a sparkly top. "Is this a bit too much?" I asked, holding it up to my chest.

Nicki stood up straight and looked me up and down. "Not if you wear it with jeans," She suggested. I examined the top carefully. I wasn't sure what kind of look I wanted to go with. I didn't want to seem like I was putting too much effort in, though I had decided to let Nicki put a little make-up on me. Only enough to hide my now dissolving stitches and maybe that mascara stuff hadn't been too bad. "I think I've got it," She grinned as she passed me some clothes. "Go try these on and I'll go ask your mum if you can borrow her boots. She's more likely to say yes to me," Nicki went off downstairs to talk to my mum, who had surprisingly been unsurprised that Jack had invited me to dinner. I tried on the clothes that Nicki had picked out. All her trousers had been discarded as we quickly figured out that though we were the same size in clothes, she was a foot taller than me and all her trousers were far too long. I put on the red top with a high waisted black skirt. The top was low cut enough to show a hint of cleavage and the skirt hugged my figure in a way that made me realise I had more curves than I had originally thought. I looked sophisticated and classy, with just a touch of danger. We had tamed my long blonde hair which I usually wore tied back and had curled it into gentle waves, which I suspected might not make it until the end of the night. I studied myself in the mirror and for once, I thought, maybe I looked a little bit beautiful.

"Bingo!" Nicki squealed as she caught sight of me. "He's going to be swept off his feet!" She smiled as she passed me the ankle boots. "Your mum has said if you scuff them you will need to buy her a new pair." Nicki rolled her eyes and started rummaging around her make-up bag. "Now sit down and keep still for a change, I need to finish this and get out of here before he turns up!"

I glanced at the time on my phone. Only half an hour and he would be here. I'd spent half the day trying to find excuses to go outside to speak to Christian, but with mum around it had been too risky. I'd spent the other half of the day wondering if I should cancel tonight. It wasn't that I didn't want to go, but in the middle of everything I was going through, did I really want to add 'dating' to that list? I couldn't help but think of the victims that had been there that night. How many of them had sat and curled their hair, and put on their make-up, not knowing it would be the last time that they ever did so? A wave of guilt swept over me. Hopefully they had all found peace on the Other Side. But for those who hadn't… How many of them would wish that they were getting ready for a night out and how many of them would be savouring every moment of being alive?

After a brief discussion with mum earlier, I had decided to take it for what it was, a nice meal out with nice company, a break away from all the madness. I had to take each moment as it came, after all, we would never know when it would be our last. It was easier said than done if I was honest to myself, but looking at how I looked right now, I was glad I was going through with it. I actually felt good about my appearance for a change.

I suppose that's what you get when you spend all day wearing hoodies with your hair scraped back. I couldn't help but wonder what Christian would think if he saw me now, a world away from the girl he had first glimpsed on a stretcher with blood caked into her hair.

Nicki finished off my make-up as I talked her out of putting any lipstick on me. "I'm going to eat and get lipstick everywhere, that's not going to look good." I huffed as she relented, how trivial it all seemed.

"Ok fine, just remember not to rub your eyes," She suggested. I turned to the mirror and smiled. With the clothes and the hair, makeup didn't look half bad on me. I actually looked like a grown-up; which seemed ridiculous for a woman who had been living on her own in London for the last year. "Right, I'm going to love you and leave you," Nicki said, giving me an air kiss as to not upset my makeup. "Relax, have a great time, then call me and tell me all about it when you get home." She grinned. "If you go home," She winked and I punched her lightly on the arm.

"Get out," I growled playfully and she danced out of the room while I straightened my skirt. With a deep breath I gathered my bag and headed downstairs to wait.

"Wow," Mum said as she closed the front door behind Nicki. "You look like a grown up," She laughed and I rolled my eyes. "Here, take this," Mum handed over a couple of £20 notes. "Always offer to split the bill," she said as I looked at her questioningly.

"Mum, don't worry about it," I said, not reaching for the money. "And this isn't my first date you know," I grumbled.

"Yes, I'm aware, but it's the first one you've been on while I'm around, so let me at least pretend I'm helping." She insisted and reached out to hand me the money.

"Fine, ok, thank you," I said as I took it and stuffed it inside my bag.

"Hey, just be grateful that I've already met this guy so I don't need to give him the third degree," Mum laughed and it made me wonder whether she'd been on many dates in the year that I was away. None that she had decided to tell me about.

"When's the last time you went out?" I asked her.

"Me? I went out to that new bar a couple of weeks ago with the girls from work," She said as started folding clothes from the washing basket.

"No, I meant, with a guy." Knowing she knew perfectly well what I meant. She had told me about guys she'd dated when I was little, but for as far back as I could remember, she'd never had a boyfriend.

"Oh, a while I guess," She shrugged. Mum had never been married, not even engaged. She'd always said we were a perfect little family, just us two. I had hoped when I left for London, she might try to find someone, but it had never happened apparently. What was she so afraid of?

"Maybe you should get out there too? Nicki told me about some great dating apps that she uses," I suggested casually, helping her pair up some socks.

Mum laughed. "I'm not sure there are many people my age on those things. Don't worry about me, I'm not lonely or anything if that's what you're thinking."

I shrugged. "No, just thought it would be a good opportunity for me to poke fun at you," I laughed and let the topic slide. I'd almost finishing pairing socks when there was a ring at the door. I glanced at my phone, right on time. After a quick check in the lounge mirror I went to the front door.

"Good luck," Mum whispered as she scurried off to hide in the kitchen.

"Hi Jack," I smiled as I opened the door. He looked even better than I remembered. He wore a shirt and a blazer with jeans and nice shoes. His blonde hair was a little shorter than when I last saw him and he'd got even taller and broad shouldered.

"Hi Emily, really nice to see you again, you look lovely," He smiled and from behind his back he presented me with a bouquet of flowers.

"Wow, that's so sweet," I said and took the flowers from him. "Erm, I'll just pop these in the Kitchen and we'll head straight out.

He got me flowers, I mouthed to my mum excitedly as I got into the kitchen, waving the flowers about. *Wow* she mouthed back and took them off me, giving me the thumbs up. I almost skipped back to the door.

"Ok so where are we going?" I asked casually as we got into his car.

"Do you remember that little Italian place that we went to for your sixteenth birthday?" He asked.

"Oh, yes I love that place!" I grinned at him, wondering whether he had really remembered or whether Nicki had given him a poke in the right direction. I decided to give him the benefit of the doubt.

When we got out of the car, he opened my door for me, and again opened the door at the restaurant and pulled out my chair. After I opened my menu, I panicked a little. I wanted pasta, but it was too messy to eat. Sauce could go everywhere, but then pizza wasn't much safer. I could eat it with a knife and fork, but would that look like I was trying too hard? Damn this delicious food.

"I think I might go for the pesto," Jack mused aloud.

"That sounds good," I said politely as my eyes scanned the menu. The pomodoro would have to wait until next time, it would have to be pizza. "I think I'll have the four-cheese pizza," Damn, was four cheeses a bit too much cheese? Did that seem greedy?

"Are you still a vegetarian?" Jack asked.

I shook my head "No, too many different and delicious food places in London, but if I can avoid eating meat I generally will." I replied.

After we ordered our food, Jack told me about his upcoming interview and the things he'd been doing to prep for it while I fiddled with my hair that I wasn't used to being down. As our food was placed in front of us, I thought about Christian and how he'd never eaten pizza. I remembered how I had hugged him and if it had been possible to hug him, then it would be possible to kiss him. If it was possible to kiss him then wouldn't it be possible for him to eat something? Could he concentrate enough to pick up pizza and put it in his mouth? Would it taste of anything? I decided I would ask him as I absentmindedly went to pick up my fork and missed it. Confused I went to pick it up again, looking down, my hand went straight through the table, missing the fork. As if it wasn't there at all. I froze.

"Everything alright?" Jack asked. "That is the right pizza isn't it?" He asked. I looked up, a stunned expression on my face.

"Yes, sorry, I was just trying to remember the last time I ate here, but it must have been on my birthday that you remembered." I forced a laugh and took a deep breath. Casually I placed my hand down on the solid table. I felt it beneath my palm, then inched my fingers towards my fork. Metal. Hard, cold metal. Gingerly, I picked up the fork that moments ago I could not. My hand shook slightly. What had just happened? I took another deep breath to steady my shaking and began to cut up the pizza. Everything was fine. Just fine.

For the rest of the night I tried to concentrate on what Jack was saying, but my mind kept wandering. He said something about moving out of his parents and getting a flat with a friend. It would depend on the new job. Something else about a football team. I tried to look like I was listening whilst nodding but I knew I looked distracted.

"Listen, Emily, are you ok? Is this too soon? Being out in a public place like this?" Jack asked earnestly.

"I'm sorry Jack, I've had a lot going on recently, and I really wanted to go out with you, but I guess I'm not all there." I responded truthfully, my eyes darting to the door.

"It's fine, honestly, maybe next time we just go to yours and watch a movie? Something a bit more casual?" He asked. I was a little relieved that he still wanted a next time, but right now, I just wanted to go home and talk to Christian. I nodded and tried to smile. "Ok, you finish up, I'm just going to nip to the toilet and then we can get going," He reassured me, and I smiled gratefully as he got up to leave.

I had honestly not been able to touch that fork. Was I going crazy? Is that what had happened with the remote control the other day, had it just passed straight through me like I was some sort of ghost? A shiver went down my spine.

"Ok, let's get going," Jack said as he came back to the table.

"Ok, shall we get the bill?" I asked, eager to get up.

"It's ok, I've already dealt with it." He waved me off as he pulled out the chair for me.

"Oh Jack, you didn't have to do that, I know I've been a crappy date tonight," I said apologetically.

"Don't be silly, you've been lovely company," He lied politely as he helped me with my coat.

As we walked across the large deserted carpark, I had the feeling of being watched. Tiny pinpricks across the back of my neck that stopped me in my tracks. Jack was a few steps ahead before he realised I had stopped. He looked around quickly before coming back to me.

"Everything ok?" He asked, concerned. I nodded but said nothing and did not carry on walking. My eyes darted around the carpark. No one that I could see, but it was dark now. Plenty of shadows to hide behind. Jack took my hand and pulled me forward slightly. "Come on," He insisted. "The car is just over there," He said nodding to the end of the carpark. I took a few small steps then froze as I saw it. Deep, thick black smoke rising from the ground, right underneath my feet.

"Run," I said quickly and pulled his hand as we ran towards the car. Jack asked no questions as he ran with me. I looked behind, the smoke was chasing after us, getting thicker, moving like smoke but looking more and more like sludge. The smoke and sludge merged together, combining until it made a face, grotesque and disgusting, it dragged its smoky sludge body across the ground to us. It dragged itself over the recycling bins, pulling them down as it got closer, dragging stones and debris with it. It can touch things. It can move things. If it can touch that then it could touch me. I didn't know much about this new life, but one thing was for certain, I did not want that touching me.

"Open the door!" I almost screamed as we approached the door, Jack looked back in horror. He might not be able to see the smoke sludge ghost, but he could most likely see the recycling bins falling over and being dragged and the stones of the car park moving towards us. He fumbled with his keys unlocking the door quickly. "Drive!" I practically shouted as we got in and slammed the doors, then we sped off as fast as Jack could manage. I didn't dare look in the rear-view mirror to see if it was following.

CHAPTER 15

"Was that some sort of earthquake?" Jack asked in horror as he sped away from the scene. I gulped down a lump in my throat. I had dragged Jack into this. It was all my fault.

"Not an earthquake," I shook my head, letting my curled hair cover half my face. How could I possibly begin to explain? "I'm so sorry Jack, I shouldn't have gone out with you tonight. It wasn't right. Things are going on with me right now and it's just not safe to be around me." My heart was still pounding in my chest, but I couldn't look behind me. I couldn't see it again. If I saw it, I would scream and it's the last thing that Jack needed.

"Is it because of the terrorist attack?" Jack asked in small voice. "Are they still after you?" His voice shook slightly, and I almost wanted to laugh. I wished it were as simple as that. I could go into hiding and they might never find me. This attacker always would.

"No, it's not a terrorist," I sighed and then doubted my words. In a way, it almost was a terrorist. "I can't explain it, I'm sorry. Just get me home, please." I said, feeling a lump in my throat again.

As he pulled up outside my house, I took a moment to look around. I couldn't see anything that I wasn't meant to. As I opened the door, he got out too and followed me to my door. I couldn't bear to stand outside and say goodnight. "Come on in," I said as we approached the door and I got out my keys. The lights were off, looks like mum was already in bed. I clicked on the lamp and led Jack to the kitchen, which gave the illusion of privacy. I turned to speak to Jack, but he beat me to it.

"We've known each other for years Emily. We may have never been close, but I would like to be. I'd like to think I could be someone that you trust, someone that you could confide in." Jack paused but I said nothing. "I'm sorry, I'll just go." He shook his head and turned to leave.

"No, wait Jack." I said quickly. "I do want to trust you, but you have to understand something. This is all very new to me and it's..." I faltered and looked at the ceiling. "It's stuff I haven't even told my mum yet." Anxiously I chewed on my bottom lip as I debated what to tell him, or if I could. "Look, you can laugh at me if you want, or you can walk out that door and never talk to me again. Or go and sell the story to some trashy magazine, I'm sure they'd pay a bunch. But ever since the attack last week, I had some sort of... brush with death. And now, I'm seeing spirits. Not just seeing them but talking to them and one... one is even sort of my friend. But there is good and bad out there and tonight I saw some of the bad stuff, it followed me and could still be following me. We're safe here, but I've still got a lot to figure out and I can't be dragging anymore people in this." I sighed and looked up at him. His expression seemed guarded.

"Emily, if you don't want to tell me what's really going on..." Jack began.

"Don't you dare tell me I'm making this up," I snapped at him. "This isn't some story just to get rid of you. You told me you wanted me to trust you and this is your chance. If you don't believe it then you can ask Nicki. But this is real, and it's scary, and I don't want to mix you up in it." I finished and crossed my arms. Jack looked at me for a moment, as if he was battling his beliefs between what's real and what isn't in his head.

"I want to believe you," He said carefully. "But you've got to admit it all seems rather... out there," I shook my head. I knew that telling anyone else wasn't going to be as easy as telling Nicki. All thoughts about telling my mum went straight out my head.

"You don't have to believe it, you just have to believe that right now, I'm not safe, and whatever this was, it's not good for you." I sat down awkwardly on the breakfast bar stool.

"Ok, look, I'm not saying I believe in ghosts or anything like that. But I believe that you believe what you saw, and I hope that's good enough for you, for now. But I'm not going to laugh at you, or storm off, or tell anyone. This remains safe with me," He answered honestly. "Maybe I could even help."

I snorted unattractively. "Everyone wants to help." I rolled my eyes, all attempt at manners gone. "Please, just go." I asked him. He waited for a moment.

"Goodnight Emily," and with that, Jack left.

When I heard the front door close, I got up and went to the back door then froze with my hand on the handle. It could still be out there; it could have followed me home. It didn't before, but it knew I had Christian with me and there was no Christian there tonight. Was he here somewhere, waiting for my call? Had he seen me arrive home? My fear between seeing the smoke ghost and my need to talk to Christian battled it out in my head. If I waited until the morning, mum would be up and it would be impossible to speak to him privately and I couldn't wait until the weekend was over, it would be the longest Sunday of my life.

"Emily?" I heard a voice call. Christian. I opened the door.

"Christian," I sighed. Tears began to roll down my face.

"What is wrong?" He asked, coming closer to the door, but not touching the threshold. I remained in the safety of the house. All I really wanted was for him to hold me, but fear rooted me to the kitchen floor. I shook my head as I took deep breaths trying to calm myself. "Did he hurt you?" Christian suddenly asked, anger flashed on his face.

"No," I said quickly. "No, not him. I saw it again, outside the restaurant, but it was worse this time. More solid, it had a *face*. It could *touch* things; it tipped the recycling bins over as it went past and dragged things along the floor as it moved. It was *hor-*

rible." I choked out as I tried to swallow my tears.

"I have been here all-night Emily, it is not here, it did not come home with you, you are safe," Christian insisted. I took a trembling step out the door and fell into his arms. He held me as large, body racking sobs ripped through my throat, my body was shaking as all the emotion I had bottled up came spilling out at once. As I quietened, letting the last feeble tears fall from my face, Christian picked me up and placed me the chair on my patio, I mildly wondered what it would look like to a passer-by, whether it would look like I was floating. I felt the warmth of him fade away as he let go of me and knelt close. "We will find this thing, and we will find a way to get rid of it. I *promise*." He whispered. I nodded and wiped my face with the back of my hand. So much for not rubbing at my eyes.

"There's more," I stated as I took a few more deep breaths to make sure the crying had really finished. "Something is happening to me. It happened the other night I think, but I wasn't sure, but tonight I'm sure it *did* happen." I took another breath, steading myself. "I went to pick up my fork for dinner and my hand went *through* the table. Straight through. I couldn't pick it up. Same with the remote control the other night, it just fell through my hands, almost like I was a ghost." I hiccupped, not bothering to correct myself. I watched the uncertainty in Christian's eyes, like he wasn't sure whether he had heard me correctly.

"So, you could not pick up anything? Did your friend see?" Christian asked. I shook my head.

"No, it was only for a moment and then I was ok." I told him. Christian looked at the floor, puzzlement on his face, like he was trying to work something out. "What does it mean?" I asked him hopefully. Christian opened his mouth to speak, then shut it again and slowly shook his head.

"Some kind of intermittent transparency perhaps. Perhaps with a trigger you can switch on and off." Christian stood up and paced around the garden. He turned back to me. "Was there something you were doing or thinking when it happened?" He asked. I frowned, trying to think back, then looked up at him.

"I think... I think I was thinking about you." I answered slowly. Christians eyebrows furrowed and he came back and stood by me.

"There is still so much we do not know about what happened to you, about what *is* happening to you. I was not lying when I told you that I had never met anyone like you before Emily, and I have been around. There may be more to this than we think." His concerned expression worried me.

"What does any of that mean? Am I turning into a ghost?" I asked, the lump returning to my throat as I choked out the word 'ghost'. Christian shook his head again.

"No, I do not think so, not in so many words. I think your ability to see into the Inbetween is not your only ability. I think you might be able to touch it as well. If you concentrate maybe. Just like I have to concentrate to touch your world. Perhaps connecting with me in your thoughts makes it easier for you to do that, which is a good thing because it means you can control it." He knelt back down beside me.

"Are you sure?" I asked, it sort of made sense. In a way.

"Not at all," He gave me his half smile. "But it makes sense to me, it makes sense that I can seem to touch you much more easily than I can touch anything else. Less concentration needed, if you are already part way in this world. Maybe it is why I seem more alive to you," Christian stood up and looked around the garden, he paused for a moment then picked up a small gardening spade and placed it on the table in front of me. "We can test it," He suggested.

"I don't want to," I said in small, scared voice.

"Emily, if we test it, we can see if the theory is correct, if it is then I can teach you how to use it and how to control it." Christian gently cupped her chin and turned her face towards him. "If you can control this, then you might be able to control more than you think. Including that smoke spirit." He told me softly. I nodded with my chin still in his hand. He smiled, took his hand away and looked down at the spade.

Shivering from the cold of the air and the remainder of my crying episode, I looked at the spade cautiously. I closed my eyes and tried to concentrate, then lowered it down and picked up the spade. I peeked open one eye. The spade was very much in my hand. I put it back down. "I don't know what I'm doing, I don't know how to willingly do this," I sighed. Perhaps it didn't really happen in the restaurant. Perhaps I was tired and my mind was playing tricks on me. And yeah, maybe I really wasn't talking to a hundred-year-old ghost either, I wanted to roll my eyes at myself.

"Think of me," Christian suggested softly. "If you were thinking of me before, think of me now. We have this connection, you and me. I know that you feel it too. That connection can make you stronger if you let it." His words made tingles go up my spine and unwillingly a smile came to my lips. I looked at the spade. I remembered our embrace, earlier that day. Not when I had fallen into his arms crying, but when I was happy, pleased we'd come up with a solution to a problem. The strength of his arms around me and the warmth that I felt from him, the safety that I had found within his arms. Slowly, but determined, I swooped down to grab the spade, willing myself to believe that my hand would go straight through it. And it did. I yelped in surprise and a little bit of fear. Adrenaline shot through my veins and Christian beamed like a proud teacher.

"I did it," I gasped, unwilling to try it again in case I failed.

"You did," Christian smiled. "And it will only get easier, the more connected you get to this world, the easier it will be for you to control. You are so much stronger than you think Emily,"

He said with glee in his voice.

"I still don't really understand how this can help me," I said helplessly, not really understanding his joy.

"For every action there is an opposite reaction." Christian stated. "If you can learn to be able to go through solid objects on this side then you can learn to not let other things touch *you* in the Inbetween. There might be more too it, more power here that you haven't tapped into yet, but for the moment I would settle for making sure you are safe from the smoke spirit." He said. So, it wouldn't be able to touch me. Wouldn't be able to paralyse me. I could learn to make sure it could have no power over me at all. A slow smile reached my face. "Not to mention," Christian continued. "You could learn to walk through walls." He laughed and I couldn't help but laugh with him.

CHAPTER 16

I woke to my phone buzzing underneath my pillow. I slapped my pillow, searching with my hand with my eyes still closed. I peeped open one eye to look at who was calling then lazily accepted the call. I grunted instead of saying hello.

"So, you didn't call me last night," Nicki said, far too loudly. "And when you didn't respond to any of my texts, I text Jack. Then he called me. What the hell happened?" She practically shouted down the phone. I grunted again and turned over to my other side and lay my phone on my ear.

"I had to tell him," I said softly, closing my eyes. "That smoke thing came back, worse this time. He saw stuff I couldn't explain." I told her.

"Ok, just back up, I need more detail than that," She asked. I groaned and sat up and rubbed my eyes. Black mascara came away on my fingers, I'd forgotten to take my makeup off and probably resembled a panda. I then went on to describe to Nicki exactly what had happened, leaving out the part of my disappearing hand and anything that happened after Jack left.

"He freaked out and left. Not that I blame him, but it just proves that I've got to stay put until I figure some things out, I don't know what I was thinking, going out on a date like that. Stupid of me." I finished.

"Dude, he didn't freak out! He was surprised, yes, and perhaps a little doubtful, but come on, wouldn't you be?" Nicki asked.

"He practically told me I was making it up just to get rid of him!" I exclaimed, fully awake now.

"Oh, come on," Nicki continued. "If Jack had just told you he had seen a flying a pig, would you have believed him?"

"If I had just seen something large flying through the sky I might have," I told her.

"Yeah ok, but he didn't see what you saw. He saw bins falling over and gravel moving towards him. Your brain would automatically try and explain that away with science rather than fantasy. You'd been off with him all night and distant, then you invite him into your home, told him you see dead people. Give the guy a break, it's not an easy thing to digest." Nicki scolded me.

I lay back on my pillows. Maybe I had been a little harsh, but last night I didn't care whether he believed me or not. I was just scared and confused. "Ok, yes, you're right," I gave in.

"Look, I filled him in with what's been happening, I told him about Grams and I told him I believe it, all of it, and I think he's coming round to the idea." Nicki said.

"Oh, so he believes you and not me." I grumbled.

"Oh, come on! It's much easier to believe the same story from two people than it is from one. If I had been the one to tell him and he went to you for confirmation, then it would have been you he believed. Bottom line is, he's coming around to the idea, I think he just needs some time to really come to terms with it all. And for the record, he's not going to tell anyone." Nicki finished.

"I know, I know. He's a decent guy, but I don't even think I've come to terms with it all yet. I should apologise to him," I sighed.

"I don't think he wants an apology Emily, I think he just wants to be there for you. Just, give him a few days and then maybe give him a call?" Nicki suggested.

"Yes, ok fine," I agreed.

"You're a muppet, you know that right?" Nicki said, I could hear her smile.

"Yes, I know," I agreed again, and we said our goodbyes.

My problem was that I had spent most of my teenage years with a crush on Jack, and I had always resigned myself to the fact that it wasn't going to happen. He was sweet, and kind and good looking, never had a bad word to say about anybody. He was the kind of guy that most girls fancied but would never dream of doing anything about it because he was so out of anyone's league. And now he finally wanted to be something more in my life, it was just at the worst possible timing. Unfortunately, that wasn't just due to having one foot in the Inbetween, but also down to Christian. I tried to shake my head to remove thoughts of him, just in case it caused my hairbrush to fall through my disappearing hands. I did have to get some sort of control over it all though. I couldn't just stop thinking about him, but I couldn't risk not being able to pick up a toothbrush either.

Whilst mum made breakfast, I answered her questions about my date vaguely. Yes, it was nice, he was a gentleman, paid for dinner, walked me to my door. No, no goodnight kiss, probably not ready for anything just yet to be honest. The answers seemed to satisfy her curiosity.

I checked my e-mails while eating, I had roughly half the amount of replies from journalists that I had e-mailed out to. I was a little impressed, considering it was the weekend. I scrolled through their offers and their terms, deciding I would have to add a term to the list. Must be done in my home. No way was I going to an interview and freaking out if a smoke spirit was going to pop out. It might make for good tv, but I had no desire for that kind of fame. I read out some of the offers to mum.

"Worth holding out until the rest of them respond once they're back in the office," Mum told me.

"Yes, I'm in no rush," I agreed as I swallowed the rest of my orange juice and headed back upstairs. I got out my phone and searched through the contacts until I found Frankie's number.

"Hi Frankie, it's Emma, we met at the spirit group the other day?" I said quietly.

"Oh yes, Emma! How are you? We worried about you after you left." Frankie said, a little cautiously.

"Yes, I wanted to apologise for that, I didn't realise how sensitive I would be to it all, I don't think I'm quite ready for all of this yet, I might just need a little time," I answered honestly.

"Yes, perfectly understandable," She said quickly, obviously quite relieved that I wouldn't be coming back.

"Erm, Frankie, the woman that I was sitting next to, not my friend, but the other side... The one who said that she could feel something and then I freaked out... I wondered if I could have her number at all? I'd love to be able to contact her and apologise for what happened, I don't want her thinking it's her fault." I said hopefully.

"Oh, my dear, I'm sure she doesn't think that, these things can happen. Everyone's contacts are on the Facebook group for those who are happy to send them. Do you want me to invite you to it?" She asked and I paused. My name on my Facebook account was not the one that I had given her.

"Erm, I actually don't have a Facebook account, more of an Instagram girl personally," I tried to laugh gently. "Do you mind having a look for me?"

"Right ok, just one moment," She seemed a little put out, but if she was going to invite me to the group anyway, why not just spend an extra two seconds getting up the contact information? I tried to bite down on my thoughts, she was helping me after all. "Right here it is, have you got a pen?" I put her on loudspeaker as I typed the number into my phone. "Her name is Angela, I'll drop her a message, so she knows to expect a call from you," Frankie told me. Warn her more like.

109

"Great, thank you for your help," I said quickly and hung up the phone before any sarcastic comments could spill out onto the phone.

*

I spent the next few days building up the courage to call Angela. After my disaster with Jack, I wasn't eager to spill out the truth to anyone else. I spent the days receiving more e-mails from journalists with more and more offers. I had e-mailed them back letting them know who the highest bidder was currently, to see if they could raise their offer. I also spent a lot of time with Christian, who was eager to teach me how to touch the Inbetween. We'd spend the mornings practising and the afternoons reading together. The practising was always exhausting – using Christian as a catalyst for my emotions to pour into not being able to touch things, and while he was next to me, the distraction of his warmth was always a challenge. I hadn't called back Jack yet, but I thought of him every day, wondering how he was coping with the news that life might not be as black and white as he once thought.

Angela picked up the phone on the fourth ring. "Hi Angela, you may not remember me, my name is Emma," I said.

"I remember you," She responded gently. Well, that wasn't good.

"Great," I tried to sound positive. "Firstly, I just wanted to apologise for what happened, I didn't mean to freak out like that." I said, trying to sound sincere.

"I understand, the first contact with the Other Side can be disturbing for some," She said, her voice almost musical, nothing like the disgusted horror that had been in her voice last week.

"That's the thing, it wasn't my first contact. Yes, I'm new to this and it was my first spirit group, but I've seen other spirits, spoken to them, in one form or another. What appeared last week was something different. Something *bad*." I let the fear seep into my voice.

"You felt it too," Angela's voice almost seemed relieved, but quite matter of fact.

"I didn't just feel it, I *saw* it," I told her. "It was barely there, in the form of thick smoke, but it creeped up my body and felt paralysing... and I've seen it again since. Stronger this time, it had a face, but its body was made of smoke or sludge, it dragged itself towards me... I've never seen anything quite like it before." I finished, trying to describe it was like trying to describe colours to the visibly impaired.

"You see them?" She asked in hushed tones, almost in awe.

"I do," I said in a quiet voice. "Angela, I know this is a wild request, and feel free to say no. But I need someone who knows more about this than I do. I need someone who can teach me more about this. You might not be able to see them, but you felt that thing before I did. You knew he was there, and you know a hell a lot more about all of this than I do. Please... will you help me?" I asked, suddenly desperate and fearful of her rejection. She might be my only hope.

"I don't know how much help I would be," Angela told me softly, my heart sank for a moment. "But I will do what I can." Relieved, I scribbled down her address. I almost asked if I could invite Nicki to come with me, but I had to stop holding her hand, I had to be able to do this on my own. I had to be in control of this. And who knows, with Christian helping on one side, and Angela on the other, maybe I could find a way to make it all work.

CHAPTER 17

The next day I hopped on a train into Birmingham. Angela's house was only four stops away and a five-minute walk and I found it easily. I had felt safe on the train, knowing how hard Christian has to concentrate to keep in a moving vehicle, but every step of my walk from the station to her house had been difficult. Looking over my shoulder every few steps, avoiding eye contact with people. I still had no way of knowing who was alive and who was dead. Maybe it would be something that Angela could teach me, but if she couldn't see them, I didn't know how that would be possible.

I knocked on Angela's door with trepidation, when she answered the door, she looked as I remembered. Short brown hair styled into a bob, with kind green eyes. She was smaller than me but looked close to my mums age. "Please, come in," She said as she moved aside and let me enter. Her house was a three storey Victorian terrace which was bigger on the inside than it seemed on the out. She led me into her lounge which seemed tidy yet cluttered. Her shelves were filled with books and crystals and candles, amongst other things. I wanted to spend some time browsing but remembered my manners.

"This room is incredible," I told her, looking up at the tapestry that hung on the far wall and dodging the dream catcher that hung into the middle of the room.

"That's very kind of you to say," She smiled, sitting on her deep purple sofa and gesturing for me to do the same. "I've made tea if you'd like some," She offered, pulling her tea cart over from the side of the sofa.

"Thank you," I nodded as she poured in the tea and gave me a delicate teacup. I took a small sip, it was fragrant, but I couldn't decide what kind of tea it was. Something I hadn't tried before.

"So then, tell me what it is that you'd like to know," She asked, turning to face me.

I took a deep breath. So many things whirled through my mind. What would be the most important? "Well, there is actually a lot that I would like to know, but firstly, I would like to know how to protect myself. I'd like to know how to banish unwanted spirits or ward them off. I need a way to step out of my front door without feeling *afraid*." I told her.

Angela nodded. "I can help with that. There are many different ways to get rid of unwanted guests. The one thing that you need to remember, is that spirits are people. They were people in life, and they are people in death. One of the best methods I have found is communication. If you can find out why a spirit is bothering you or tell it that you want to be left alone, I find they usually won't stay where they're not wanted."

I shook my head and cut in "I get that, but this... there is no communicating with it, it just feels angry and vengeful – I mean, you felt it last week. Whatever it is, it's bad and I don't think it will give me time to sit down and have a chat about what's bothering him," I sighed.

She nodded. "Yes, I have felt bad spirits who are only after mayhem. If he knows you can see him, he may just want to frighten you, it may have been a while since he has frightened anyone. It may get lonely on the other side and he's just doing it for his own morbid entertainment. The trick with spirits like that, is to not get their attention in the first place, but since you already have, then you can wear this." Angela unclipped a necklace from around her neck and handed it to me. The band was leather, and a gold flecked brown crystal hung from the middle. "It's called a Tigers Eye. It will dim your light, make it harder for spirits to see or sense you, as long as you don't call attention to yourself." I took the necklace and inspected it.

"It's beautiful... but don't you need it?" I asked. Angela shook her head.

"I have many more, don't you worry about that. Now, if a spirit doesn't want to cross over, then that is their business. I have read that the crossover is not the same for everyone, not everyone finds peace and many worry about what awaits them in the next world, but there is a way to banish them. It's a little extreme and it should only be resorted to as a last option. You would need around four people, three at a push. If you all join hands together and share each other's energies, then you should be able to get the spirit to cross over." Angela told me. I waited a moment, to see if there was more.

"That's it? That's the extreme method? Just join hands?" I asked, a little surprised.

Angela laughed delicately. "My dear, one live person's lifeforce is worth fifty of a spirit who can touch our world. Enough lifeforce joined together, all in harmony and in unison, wanting the same thing... it can be a very powerful thing." She smiled. I raised an eyebrow, starting to doubt if I had come to the right person. "Now, let's move on to more delightful things. Have you contacted a loved one yet?" Angela asked and took me by surprise.

"Erm, no, none that have stepped forward at least." I said. "Oh, I did manage to talk to my best friend's grandmother, though that was more mistake than anything." I shrugged.

Angela laughed again lightly. "Oh dear, you cannot expect them to just come and find you. Many are quite happy in the otherworld, knowing that their loved ones are well and looked after. If you want to speak to them, then you must call for them." Angela told her.

"Oh. I got the impression that once you crossed over, then you couldn't come back?" I asked.

"Oh nonsense, of course they can, my mother is forever popping back and forth. They can't stay for long, I'm sure it's very draining for them." Angela responded. I thought of Grams and how she couldn't stay for long.

"Do you think it's possible that if a spirit decides not to cross over, and stays this side, eventually, they wouldn't be able to cross over at all?" I asked, thinking of Christian.

"Yes, I think so dear. There is so much lifeforce on this side, I think it would most likely become too difficult. You must pity those who make that choice, never in their own world, and never belonging to ours. But it can also be a gift to those who might come to you for help. If you will it, then you can send them back, just the same as banishing them. Though instead of being ripped from this world and sent spiralling into the next, it is more of a blessing when all sides want the same thing." She smiled. I froze. I could help Christian. If he still wanted to cross over, if he still wanted peace. I could be the one to help him get there. But then why did that feeling fill me with dread? Was I really selfish enough to want to keep him around, for him not to find peace? "Did you have any other pressing questions?" Angela asked. I hesitated, shifting through my questions trying to decide on the level of their importance.

"There is something I would like to know... How can you tell who is a spirit and who isn't? I'm terrified I'm going to walk down the street and start up a conversation with someone who isn't alive and not even realise it," I told Angela. Angela's lip quirked up in a half smile.

"Well you can tell by their aura of course dear!" Angela exclaimed.

"Aura? I thought that was just some hippie way of talking about someone's energy... or soul or something," I said, realising I didn't actually know a lot about what an aura was.

"Well, yes, in a way it is, but it doesn't make it any less real. Everyone has an aura, and everyone has the ability to see them, even people who aren't connected to spirits. You and I have an aura, but spirits are made up primarily of their auras – of their energy – so it is much brighter and quite different to a live person's aura." Angela explained. I creased my forehead in a frown.

"I don't see auras." I told Angela, thinking she must think me the worst person ever to have landed these kinds of gifts.

"Yes, you do," Angela smiled warmly. "You just don't realise it. Here, come with me," She said as she stood up and made her way back into the hall, I followed obediently. "It's much easier to start on a blank background, white is easier, and that room is too cluttered." She lined herself up against the cream walls in her hallway near the stairs. "Now, take a step back," She asked me and I took a couple of small steps back so that I was mostly standing in the lounge. "Now, let your eyes relax, focus on me for a second and then let your eyes wander to the edges of my head and shoulders." She instructed. I did as I was told but I had no idea what I was looking for.

"I don't get it," I mumbled, a little embarrassed.

"It's ok dear, try again, you should be able to see a little bit of a glow that surrounds me. It won't be like a bright light, just a faint outline that should be roughly about a foot wider than I am. It will outline my entire body, but you might just see it around my head and shoulders to begin with." Angela told me, patient and calming. I tried again, my eyes darting around her body. I did see *something*... a bit like a shadow but not dark. I don't think that was it however, more like a trick of the light. "Can you see something dear?" Angela asked, curious.

I shrugged. "I thought I did but I don't think that's right," I answered honestly.

"Explain it to me," She asked.

"It's like a shadow, but not a shadow. I think it's just how the light is hitting you," I told her.

"A little bit like I have a lamp behind me or beneath me?" She asked.

"I think so?" I said, very uncertain. It was difficult to explain but the more I did, the stronger it got and the clearer I saw it. "It's like a haze of light behind you, but very faint," I told her.

"That's my aura dear," Angela smiled again, pleased.

"Are you sure?" I asked, it wasn't what I imagined, not by a long shot.

Angela let out of a gentle laugh. "Yes, that's right dear. Now a spirit's aura is stronger than this, maybe brighter, and sometimes colourful. When you talk to people from now on, always try to have a look out for their aura, it's always there, easier to see on some backgrounds than others, but it will be there. The more you train your eyes to look for it, the stronger and more sensitive you will become to it, and therefore more likely to be able to tell the difference between a living person and a spirit." Angela finished and headed back into the lounge. "Now," Angela continued as she sat down crossed legged on the rug in the middle of the room. "Let us practise calling a loved one. Have you got anything with you that belonged to a deceased relative at all?" She asked as I joined her on the floor.

"Erm, no sorry, I don't. I actually don't really know that many people who have died." I told her.

"Well don't be sorry about that my dear. Not a problem, you can practise calling my mother, she won't mind." Angela gave me a toothy grin. I let my mouth hang open. I couldn't just *call* for someone's dead mother.

"You want me to just… call out for your mother?" I asked, confused and a little shocked.

"No no dear, it's not quite that simple. You need a connection, either something that belonged to them or something that they held quite dear to them when they were living." Angela leaned over to a bookcase and grabbed a small box and opened it, inside was a ring. "I use my mother's wedding ring." She smiled.

"So, I call her and she's just going to pop up in front of me? What happened to not calling attention to myself?" I asked.

"Oh, don't worry, my mother is a very lovely woman, she won't be a bother to you. I don't know about her popping up in front of you, as I'm afraid I don't get a visual, but this should be interesting for all of us." Angela leant over and passed me her mother's wedding ring and I held it cautiously. "Now, different things work for different people, you just need to find a way that works for you. You can hold the ring and call out her name, invite her into the safe space, let her know it's ok to visit. Like I said before, spirits are people, if you were tucked up cosy in another world and you heard someone calling for you, what would you like to hear? What could someone say to make you visit?"

I tried thinking for a minute, it kind of made sense but at the same time seemed completely insane. But then with all the things I had seen recently, this was quite low down on the crazy scale. Curiosity of wondering whether I would actually be able to call her mother forward got the better of me and I closed my eyes and took a deep breath. Then I peeked open one eye. "What was her name?" I asked.

"Mary," She answered, smiling.

"Right ok," I said and took another deep breath. "Mary, I would like to talk to you, I'm with your daughter Angela and she's trying to help me, I wondered if you might be able to help me too?" I called out into the lounge, holding the ring inside my closed hand. "Wait," I said and opened my eyes to look at Angela. "I know that spirits can't enter a house that you have a connection with. But my friend's Grams was able to enter her house. Can they only enter houses that they have a connection with? Does your mum have a connection to this house?" I asked.

"I certainly do," A voice came from the sofa and made me jump. I placed a hand on my rapidly beating heart. "This was my house too once. Unfortunately, it has been many people's houses, so my daughter gets a few different visitors," Mary smiled. She looked similar to Angela. I had been expecting an old woman, but she was perhaps a similar age to Angela, maybe slightly older, and her hair was longer.

"She's here," Angela smiled, following my gaze to the sofa.

"And you can't see her?" I asked. Angela shook her head.

"No, but I can feel her," Angela smiled. "Can you describe her to me?" Angela asked.

I looked back to Mary, who smiled kindly. "She looks like you," I told her. "She looks more like an older sister than a mother though," I said.

"I passed when I was only a few years older than Angela is now," Mary confirmed. I repeated it back to Angela.

"Fascinating," Angela whispered in awe, looking at me.

"Can you not hear her either?" I asked Angela, again she shook her head.

"I can get images and thoughts and stray words. Mostly I can get emotions. It must be wonderous for you," Angela told me.

I looked back towards Mary. "Are you at peace, where you are Mary?" I asked, so curious about what lay on the other side. Mary smiled again at me.

"Yes, sweet child, it is peaceful here and we are happy. I enjoy my visits to my daughter, but I know where I really belong." She replied. She did look peaceful.

"Was it easy for you to decide to cross over Mary? You didn't want to stay here in the Inbetween?" I asked.

Mary's eyes twinkled with curiosity. "You've been speaking to other spirits," She smiled. "Yes, sweet child, it was easy for me to cross over. I died in peace and now I rest in peace. It is only hard for those who are not at peace and worry what might await them on the Other Side." I nodded to show that I understood.

"So, does that mean that there is a heaven and hell?" I asked, a little scared.

Mary laughed delicately. "No, my child, there is only peace here for us. There may be something worse that waits for those who have not lived a good life, but as someone who has found peace, I cannot be sure of that." She told me.

"Does that mean," I continued, eager for more, knowing I only had a short time. "That those who find peace can come back and visit, and those who don't deserve peace go somewhere else… where they can't visit?" I asked.

"That is right," She agreed. "I have met many spirits whilst in the Inbetween, they are all spirits who found peace on the crossover, or they are spirits who decided not to cross over. I have never met a spirit who has crossed over and not found peace." She said.

"So that means, that when you cross over, there might only be peace? For everyone? No matter how they led their life? It's either peace… or the possibility of finding something other than peace scares a spirit so much they choose the Inbetween instead?" I asked, but I was mostly talking to myself. It sounded like there was no such thing as hell, just the threat of it, and that was enough to make people choose a limbo like the Inbetween instead of crossing over. Did that make peace Heaven and the Inbetween Hell? I couldn't keep the thought straight in my head.

"I'm afraid I don't have all these answers my child. Was there anything else?" She asked.

I looked back to Angela. "Angela, is there anything that you want to ask your mum outright?" I wondered aloud, if she'd only managed to contact her through words and emotion, she might not ever had the chance.

"Ah very kind of you. Yes, where is the Mariah Carey CD that I lost last month?" Angela asked. I couldn't help it, I laughed.

Mary actually rolled her eyes. "Please inform my daughter that I am not a sniffer dog and if I wasn't here when she lost it, then I don't know where it is." Mary said. Choking back laughter I repeated Mary's words. Angela looked a little put out. "I have to go," Mary told me with kind eyes.

"Thank you for your help Mary," I said, and with that, she faded away, just as Grams had done.

CHAPTER 18

The conversation with Mary had drained me but armed with new knowledge and my new necklace safely secured around my neck, I thanked Angela and headed home. I felt safer on the walk back to the train station, though a few things were bothering me. Christian was stuck in the Inbetween after staying for too long. Did he realise that he would be able to cross over and still visit for a short time? Have the best of both worlds? And if he did but was still unsure about crossing over, was it because he wasn't sure he would find peace? I decided I had to ask him about it, carefully. Maybe it was a touchy subject. He had never once mentioned how he died, or really anything to do with his life. But then I had also never asked. I also couldn't help but think about what Angela had said. I could banish bad spirits and I could help good ones. I could help spirits cross over, send them to peace, whether they wanted to or not. Though it sounded like if they didn't want to, it wouldn't be a pleasant experience. Could it really be as easy as willing them to go away? I wasn't sure. And was I ready to tell Christian about my newfound ability? Not even slightly. And, even if I did, maybe he wouldn't want to cross over just yet. Maybe he'd want to stay with me a little longer. On the train I opened my e-mails. The remaining defeat e-mails confirming that they couldn't beat the current highest bid. That was it then, confirmed. I would be starring in a live broadcast in my own lounge in perhaps just a few days' time. I felt more confident about it now, much surer that it was the right thing to do. I e-mailed back the highest bidding company and confirmed that I accepted the offer, along with my accepted questions that they had inquired about. With my stitches almost gone and my new crystal, I was about ready to take on the world.

"Christian!" I called into the garden once I got home.

"Emily?" I heard an unsure voice call back. Christian stepped closer towards the house but frowned at the open back door. "Emily?" He said again.

"I'm back," I smiled and took a step toward him.

"How are you doing that?" He asked, his voice was confused and a little concerned.

"How am I doing what?" I asked, suddenly less cheerful.

"You are... Kind of hazy," He said, a crease appearing on his forehead as he frowned, taking another step towards me. "Are you doing that?" He asked. Confused for only a moment I realised what must be going on. I reached round to the back of my necklace and pulled it off and placed it onto the patio table.

"Better?" I asked.

"Much better," He said, relief filled his voice. "What *is* that?" He asked, looking at it horrified.

"It's some kind of protection stone, it's going to help me be unnoticed by other spirits. Sorry, I should have realised that that would include you too." I shook my head. The drawbacks of having a ghost friend.

"Right ok," Christian responded, still warily looking at the stone. "Where did you get this from?"

"From that women from the spirit group I told you about," I said as I plonked my bag on the table.

"Ah ok," He said, though he didn't seem sure. "She was useful then?" He asked.

"Yeah I think so, I didn't learn much new, she basically knew what you had already told me," I shrugged, biting my lip to keep from confessing that I could help him cross over. I would tell him, at some point, when the moment was right. "Oh, but I did learn something!" I said excitedly. "Apparently I can call other spirits if I have something personal that belongs to them." I smiled.

"Oh, do you *want* to call other spirits?" Christian asking doubtfully.

"Well, not really. But it's good to know I can if I ever need to, I guess. You know, in the future, maybe when my Grandparents cross over." I shrugged, then inwardly cringed at mentioning the words 'cross over'.

"Yes, I suppose so," Christian responded. "Did you still want to practise today?" He asked. "I am thinking maybe we started practising the reverse, I try to touch your arm and you try to prevent me from touching you?" He suggested.

"That's a good idea," I nodded. "But before we do, I wanted the chance to talk to you about something. With all the talk about spirits and the cross over today, I realised that I'd never really asked you about… what happened… when you died?" I started confidently but finished in a small voice. Was it rude to ask that?

"Oh," Christian paused. "What brought that on?" He asked.

"It was nothing in particular, Angela mentioned about how her mother died and I realised I hadn't asked you about it, and I didn't want you to think I didn't care or anything, I just thought maybe it was a touchy subject, and maybe we were at the point that I could probably ask you about it," I glanced at his solemn face. "Was I wrong?" I asked shyly.

"No, not at all. I do not mind telling you, it is just… I know it is ridiculous because I am teaching you about the Inbetween, but sometimes I do not wish to remind you that I am dead." He said slowly.

"Oh," I said. "If it helps, I don't think of you like that. I don't sit here with you and think 'he's a spirit'. I just sit here and think 'I'm with my friend'," I shrugged and laughed, and it brought a small smile to his face.

"Ok well, it is not an enjoyable story, but I do not mind telling you. I just ask that you do not judge me for it." He asked, looking at me sternly.

"Ok…" I willed him to continue and took a seat.

"I was born in 1851, it was a different time, so much has changed and developed since then," He shook his head slightly and continued. "I was twenty-four when it happened. I was still living at home with my parents and my younger sister, Victoria. Father had been injured in a machinery incident, we had family money, but it was up to me to make sure things kept ticking over. My sister was five years younger than me, and she was beautiful. With money and beauty, she had the pick of any suitor she wanted. I remember that night so clearly, even though we had been drinking, because she had just agreed upon a marriage and we were celebrating. He was a fine young man, decent and well-spoken of. Later that night, while we were all sleeping, two men broke into our house," Christian paused, his voice became hushed. "They were more like monsters than men. I woke hearing my sister scream, but by the time I got to her room, she was gone… they had taken her. I raced down the stairs and I caught them before they left the building. My sister was thrown over one of their shoulders, like she was a sack of goods he could steal in the night. I tackled him. My sister was thrown to the side, the other one ran but this one I had in my hands, we struggled for only moments as he tried to get free, I slammed him so hard into the marble floor he smashed his head and never awoke. It was only afterwards when I realised what I had done, that I noticed a knife sticking out of my side. I had not even noticed it go in. I took it out automatically and the pain swept up my body all at once and brought me to my knees. I went to my sister for help, but she had been knocked unconscious by the fall. I can remember dragging myself up to the stairs to get my parents, but I passed out before I made it. They found my body in the morning, drained of blood." Christian paused and I flinched as he wiped away a tear that I hadn't realise I'd shed.

"Oh Christian, oh Christian I'm so sorry," I said. "I'm sorry I made you tell me that, I didn't know it would be so… so painful," I said as I gathered him in my arms and held him for a moment.

"Do not fret," He smiled. "I chose to watch over my sister, and I chose to teach myself to interact with your world as much as I could, so that maybe I could help her if the second man ever came back. I watched my sister and my parents grieve, then I watched her get married, and have children. Then I watched her children grow up and have children of their own, and then I got to watch over them. Unfortunately, my blood line ended during the first world war, and by that point I was too far immersed in your world." He said sadly. This might have been a good time to mention that I could help him cross over, but selfishly I kept my mouth shut. "You reminded me of her a little, at first." He told me.

"Of your sister?" I asked, not sure how I felt about that.

"Yes, Victoria was fair and slight, like you, almost my polar opposite. She was gentle and kind and *good*." He smiled. "But the more I get to know you, the more I see the differences."

"Oh," I said. "Like what?"

"You have an inner strength in you that I never saw in her. A need to survive no matter what. An eagerness to embrace life, even when your life contains death. Your compassion and understanding. The energy you have in abundance that seems to spill out of you." The corner of his lip quirked up in a smile as he tucked a loose strand of my hair behind my ear. "You are the most fierce, strong and beautiful woman I have ever seen," He whispered as he leaned in close, if he'd been alive, I would have been able to feel his breath on my skin. He leaned in closer, his intoxicating eyes searching mine desperately. In the end, it was me who closed the gap between us, as I greeted his lips with my own.

CHAPTER 19

Kissing Christian was unlike anything I'd ever done before. I felt my phone fall through my hands as I reached for him in the In-between and I couldn't tell if he was here in my world or if I was there, in his. There was no breathing or breathlessness, just us, tangled in an unending embrace.

When it did end, I felt a sudden shyness sweep over me, I looked up at him and he was beaming.

"Now that was... An experience," He smiled down at me, still holding me in his arms.

"Yes, I'm sorry, I don't know what came over me, we probably shouldn't have," I stumbled over my words, reluctantly letting go of him.

"Do not be sorry," He said, his smile wavering.

"Right, shall we get to practising?" I asked, trying to distance myself slightly. He nodded slowly.

We spent the rest of the afternoon with me attempting to not let him be able to touch me, but I failed miserably. When I wanted to not touch something, I had to really want it. And wanting Christian not to touch me was almost impossible.

*

I few days later I had six strangers stuffed inside my lounge as well as camera equipment. The day of the interview had arrived. The cameras were a lot bigger than I was expecting, the cameraman laughed when I had told him this, saying that these were their portable ones. I dreaded to think of the monstrosities they must have at the station.

I was dressed modestly and had had a lady to do my makeup to make sure I didn't look 'too washed out' on the tv. Mum was scuttling about in the kitchen, seemingly making endless cups of tea. She'd also bought 'posh' biscuits and had displayed them nicely on one of our 'good' plates. I couldn't wait for this to be over and done with.

"Right Emily, if you could just sit over here for me," a woman directed me. "Right we're just going to test the sound so if you can just talk directly to me for a moment. How are you feeling?" She asked, and I noticed that her make-up and hair were done to perfection.

"I'm a little nervous but looking forward to getting it done with to be honest," I half smiled, and she looked over towards the men behind the camera who gave her the thumbs up.

"Ok, great, if you can stay there – Tony, if you can come sit here where I am," She said as she motioned Tony forward, he had been introduced to me when they came in, he would be presenting and conducting the interview. He seemed like a nice man, in his 50's with extremely white teeth and a 'good head of hair' as my mother had put it. Tony switched places with the producer.

"Very comfy sofa," He smiled at me. "Make sure to give me a poke if I fall asleep," He joked, and I laughed politely.

"Ok, we're on in five," The producer called out to the room. My heart started beating faster as I started to doubt my decision. The room fell silent as final checks were being made. I wished I could have had Nicki here with me, but with so many people in my small house, it wouldn't have been possible.

The two cameras made slight alterations as they tried to catch my face full on as well as Tony's so they could switch back and forth as we spoke. They instructed me not to move too much as I would go out of shot – and with it being live, they wouldn't be able to fix that. There were other things they had asked for me to remember. Don't talk too fast, have clear diction, sit up straight, no fidgeting and more. I was suddenly glad I hadn't been much good at drama class and hadn't gone into acting.

"Ok this is it! We're on in 5, 4, 3, 2 and…" The producer waved her arm and pointed to Tony.

"Thank you, Rachel, yes that's right, we're here today with Beacon of Hope, Emily Anderson, the one and only survivor of the Theatre Terrorist Attack which sadly claimed over 1,100 lives. Now Emily…" Tony shifted his attention away from the camera and towards me, I felt my heart drop to my stomach as I tried to remember the questions I had agreed that he could ask and the answers I had rehearsed over and over. "The attack was over two weeks ago, firstly and foremost, how are you feeling now?" He asked.

I licked my lips slightly and tried to respond clearly. "Thank you for asking Tony, it's been a difficult couple of weeks, coming to terms with what happened, but I'm grateful to be here with my mum who has been such a pillar of support, as have my friends." I tried a shy smile but quickly decided to keep my face solemn.

"Well that's good to hear that you've had people to help you through this difficult time. I know a lot of our viewers out there are wondering what happened, and how you think you managed to survive when others didn't?" He asked. This was the big question.

"I think it was luck, more than anything. There is no real reason that I survived when others didn't," I shook my head.

"Can you tell us in your own words what happened?" Tony urged as I left the question largely unanswered.

"I was… In the bathroom when it first started, when I realised what was going on, I ran up to the foyer to get outside, but they'd put down the lock gate and we couldn't get it up. I rang 999 but they had already received a call and they were on their way. The operator asked me if there was anywhere safe I could hide, but by that point, everyone was running, and you could hear the gunmen were everywhere. There was nowhere safe. So, the operator told me to play dead. I think it was her, and luck, that saved my life." I swallowed a lump in my throat. "It was then that I fell down, hitting my head and making it bleed. I had other people fall on top of me, half covering me, maybe that is another reason I survived. The gunmen were checking on the wounded and trying to ensure that there were no survivors. I stayed still, as long as I could, trying not to flinch when I heard them come near me. At some point, I passed out, probably from hitting my head and when I woke up next, I was in the hospital," I lied. I had got through the worst part.

"It sounds horrendous Emily, that must have been awful for you." Tony said sympathetically.

"It was," I agreed. "But it's still not as awful as what happened to everyone else, and every day I wonder why I am alive, when others aren't. It doesn't seem fair to me. Every day I wonder, what if I had just grabbed someone, and told them to play dead too, would they still be alive today?" I shook my head sadly.

"In a situation like that, I know it can be easy to blame yourself or wish you had done more, but with them shooting the bodies just in case, you can't know that they wouldn't have shot them. Please Emily, I would like to think I speak on behalf of the nation when we tell you, you could not have done more. It was a horrible, harrowing attack that took place, and that you are alive at all today is a miracle." Tony told me softly. For a moment I wondered whether he had always prepared to say this, or whether it came from the heart.

"Thank you, Tony, that means a lot to me." I said with a grateful smile.

"Is there anything else you would like to tell us, about what happened that night?" He asked, getting back on track.

"Yes, I just wanted everyone to know, when I was there, and everyone was panicking and running, there were people who still stopped to help people, to help them run or to help them hide. I slipped when running up the stairs and instead of pushing past me to get ahead, a woman stopped to steady me and help me up the stairs. This dreadful thing was happening but through it all, the victims that day all died as heroes in my eyes. They still had their humanity and they were *good* people. That is why I would like to encourage everyone to donate towards the Victims of the Theatre Terrorist Attack, they all deserve a send-off worthy of heroes and they deserve to rest in peace." I said, directly to the camera.

"Yes, that's right," Tony continued. "As you know today, Emily has donated a huge amount towards this fund and with your help, not only will the victims receive the send-off that they deserve but their families will also get the support that they need to help them through this troubling time." Tony told the camera. "Well Emily, what do you think is next for you?" Tony asked.

"To be honest, I haven't decided yet. My job and my flat are still waiting for me in London, but I think I'm going to stay in Birmingham for a while longer," I told him.

"Well, we wish you the very best for the future Emily," Tony concluded.

"Thank you, Tony," I finished.

"Ok now we're back to the studio with Rachel McKindley with the remainder of today's news," Tony smiled at the camera.

"Andddd we're out!" Called the producer and everyone set in motion at once.

"Thank you, Emily," Tony shook my hand. "That can't have been easy," He said.

"You made it a lot easier," I smiled and he smiled back.

It took another hour for them to set down the equipment and to leave the house, but the room seemed suddenly very empty once they had gone.

"I'm so proud of you," Mum whispered as she hugged me from behind.

I shook my head. "Nothing to be proud of, I just did what needed to be done," I sighed, feeling like a fraud. Had the families of the victims watched that? Were they at home, hating me for being alive when their loved ones were not?

"I disagree, you didn't have to do it, but you've given the world a shred of hope in this dark time." Mum responded.

I groaned and smiled. "Don't you start calling me a beacon of hope now," I laughed, swatting at her affectionately, mum caught my hand and gave it a squeeze.

"Oh, your phone rung while you were filming by the way, but I didn't answer it." She told me.

"Oh, who was it?" I asked.

"Jack," Mum answered.

"Ah," I said. Jack. I hadn't forgotten about him, it was just that things had developed quite quickly, and even with all my apparent spare time, I hadn't had time to call him. "I'm guessing he wasn't watching the news then," I laughed.

"He can watch it on catch-up," Mum laughed back as I went into the kitchen to retrieve my phone. Time to woman-up and speak to Jack.

"Hey Jack," I said as he answered the phone after the first ring.

"Hi Emily, thanks for calling me back. Look, I owe you an apology," He started but I cut him off.

"No, you really don't. I'm the one that dumped all that information on you and then told you to leave. I'm really sorry, that was pretty shitty of me," I said.

"Yeah but you wouldn't have asked me to leave if I hadn't reacted the way that I did. I'm so sorry," He apologised.

"Water under the bridge?" I suggested. We could apologise to each other forever.

"That sounds good to me. So…" He hesitated and I heard him take a deep breath. "I was wondering maybe I could come over tomorrow night, maybe watch a movie? I'll get us in a takeaway," He offered. I paused; I hadn't been expecting that.

"Erm… Tomorrow?" I asked, stalling for time. I couldn't very well tell him I was going out.

"Yeah, or tonight if that works better for you? I've got some news." He said, I could almost hear the desperation in his voice. I suppose it wouldn't hurt to just watch a movie.

"No, tomorrow is fine – about 6?" I asked.

"Ok great, see you then," He said and hung up before I had the chance to change my mind.

"So… You're seeing Jack tomorrow?" Mum asked, earwigging.

"Yeah…" I answered unsurely.

"Em, if you're not interested, it might just be easier to put the guy out of his misery." Mum told me.

"It's not that I'm not interested. It's just, with everything going on at the moment, I'm just not sure I'm in the right head space right now." I told her.

"Yeah, I get that, but you've liked this guy for about forever, and now he's available and interested… you might not get a second chance," She warned me. I bit my tongue and thought about Christian, how could I explain to her? I could barely explain it to myself. It almost felt like I was cheating on him but it's not like we could actually ever be together in that way. It was an impossible situation.

"Mum… have you ever liked a guy when you knew it wouldn't work?" I asked slowly. Mum narrowed her eyes.

"I'm guessing we're not talking about Jack here?" She asked. I shook my head. "Ah, so that's why the sudden disinterest," Mum laughed. "There's another guy on the scene. From London?" She asked. I nodded again, averting my gaze. "Let me guess… he's gorgeous and mysterious and you know that he's bad for you, but you want him anyway?" She asked. I raised my eyebrows.

"Pretty much, how did you know?" I asked.

"Because at some point or another there is always a guy that drives you crazy in all the right ways. Let me tell you right now, he's going to break your heart." Mum half laughed. I frowned; how dare she just assume that?

"How would you know? You haven't even been with anyone since Dad left," I spat out bitterly and regretted it instantly. Mum looked surprised and a little hurt.

"Doesn't mean I haven't had my fair share of heartbreak Emily," Mum said in a low voice.

"I'm sorry," I said quickly. "I didn't mean anything by it." Just an intense feeling of protection towards Christian. "I don't think he's going to break my heart; we're just destined to fail and that's not fair on either of us I suppose," I said sadly. Mum put her arm around me and guiltily I accepted her embrace.

"You're young Em, now is the time to make these mistakes. Follow your heart, only you know what is best for you," Mum gave me a squeeze and went to the dishwasher to load the empty tea mugs.

I did know what was best for me. Jack would make a wonderful boyfriend; he would be kind and caring and a pillar of strength when I needed it. But Christian is… Christian. But he is also *dead* Christian.

I decided to ring Nicki to tell her about my date with Jack, and ask for her to come over tomorrow, with more clothes. I had hoped that I would feel like a weight had been lifted, once I had done the interview. I thought that I would be a step closer to getting my life on track, but would it ever really be back on track? Was worrying about Christian and Jack just a distraction from worrying about what was really going on? I still had to figure out where I was going to live and how I was going to pay my bills, let alone figure out how to live with one foot in the Inbetween.

CHAPTER 20

The next morning, I was in the garden with Nicki and Christian.

"Ok, what is it that you wanted to show me?" Nicki asked warily. I exchanged a mischievous look with Christian.

"Ok, don't freak out ok?" I told her as I lined up my body with the fence that joined the secluded corner of the end of our street.

"I think I've seen enough in the last few weeks to be given a little credit that I won't freak out," Nicki rolled her eyes. She hadn't loved the suggestion of hanging out in the garden with a ghost. I flashed her a smile and lifted my arms at the elbows and put my palms facing the fence. I took a deep breath. *I can walk through this fence.* I closed my eyes. I'd been practising and practising and was at the point that I thought I could finally show Nicki without making a mistake.

I can walk through this fence. I took another deep breath and took a step forward. I heard Nicki gasp and I opened my eyes; I was through the other side. I quickly turned around and walked back through the fence, reappearing in front of Nicki. Christian cheered and Nicki looked wide eyed, a hand dramatically covering her wide opened mouth.

"How did you *do* that?" Nicki gasped, shaking her head.

"Yeah, I can walk through walls now," I smiled, sharing a thankful glance with Christian. I wouldn't ever have been able to do it without his help. I wasn't sure when or how it would come in handy, but it was nice to feel I had some control of this aspect of me now, rather than the other way around. I turned to Nicki and her face was filled with horror.

"Emily, I didn't see you walk through the fence," Nicki told her.

"Erm, yeah you did," I told her. "I just walked through and came back again. You saw me, you were right there. You gasped and everything," I said, confused.

"No Emily," She told me quietly. "I didn't see you walk through the fence; I saw you *disappear*," She said, her voice filled with horror. I looked at Christian, but he looked just as confused as I felt.

"I disappeared?" I said, still looking at Christian, and I watched the realisation dawn on his face.

"When your hand is going through things, or when you're walking through walls, you must completely step into the Inbetween to do that. I didn't realise, because I can see you in your world and in the Inbetween… but normal people can't." He told me.

"Oh wow…" I said. "That's even better! I can completely disappear!" I laughed. Nicki did not seem as pleased.

"What does this mean Emily? How is it that you're able to do that?" She asked.

"No, it's ok, honestly. It's just a part of the whole ghost seeing experience. I've got one foot in the Inbetween now, it means I can see and interact with it like a spirit can. It's a good thing Nicki, it means I can learn to defend myself against dark spirits." I told her. I watched as Nicki digested this information. "It freaked me out too at first, but it's not like I can help it, so I may as well try and get control of it. Christian has been helping me," I told her. I saw a flash of doubt cross her face, but she covered it quickly.

"Ok just don't… step into the Inbetween and never come back ok?" She asked, her voice quivered slightly.

"No don't worry, I can't even hold it for very long I don't think. It took Christian years to teach himself how to do it." I laughed, not understanding her worry. I suppose if I tried to see if from her side, it was pretty scary. She would just need some time to adjust, just like I had.

"Right ok, sure." She said as she watched me smile in the area that Christian was standing. Must be strange for her to watch me smile and talking to a person that she couldn't see. "Right, I thought we were going to go to the shops before we choose what clothes you're going to wear for your date tonight? We have to go more casual this time by the way," she said.

"Yes, right ok," I said quickly, hoping Christian hadn't heard.

"Date?" Christian asked solemnly.

"It's just Jack. We're just watching a movie," I told him, trying to make it sound casual. I don't know why; did I really have to offer him an explanation?

"Of course. Enjoy," He said and disappeared in the blink of an eye.

"What's wrong?" Nicki asked as I looked sadly at the ground where he had been standing.

I shook my head. "I think Christian is a little upset. He's gone." I stated, trying to look like it didn't bother me.

"It's only normal for him to be jealous Emily," Nicki told me.

"He's not jealous," I said as I headed inside.

"Of course, he is," Nicki said, following me. "You're literally his whole world. He probably hates having to share you with me and your mum, God knows how he feels when you throw a good looking male into the mix," Nicki scoffed. A part of me knew she was right, in a way, I really was his whole world. But Nicki didn't know there was more to it than that now.

"Let's get me dressed," I told her, trying to change the subject. Mine and Christian's inappropriate feelings for each other could wait for now.

*

Nicki sighed as we wandered down the busy high street. "I don't get it, if we're not actually going to buy anything, then what are we doing here?" She asked.

"I told you," I rolled my eyes at her. "I'm looking for auras," I smiled, as if it was the most normal thing in the world.

"Yeah ok, but can we do that *and* buy clothes?" She asked and stuck her tongue out at me.

"There aren't as many people in shops, I need a good crowd," I told her then was rooted to the spot for a moment as I spotted a man all in black with his hood up. For an instant, my veins seemed to be filled with ice as my body went cold. A flicker of a man in a black hoodie with a black ski mask covering his face flashed through my mind and bile rose in my throat. The man in black turned for a second as he reached for his earphones and my body seemed to start working again. He was just a teenager. No threat here, no fear. I gulped down a lump in my throat as I tried to regain my composure. I tried to see if I could find his aura, but even looking at the back of his black hoodie made my body want to run. He *did* seem to have an aura, but did his aura seem different? I had managed to spot some auras of people that seemed a little brighter and busier, but they had always turned out to be alive. And I couldn't see everyone's auras yet. People kept moving and with the busy background it was difficult to really grab at. "What about him?" I subtly jerked out my chin at the man by the bus stop. Nicki glanced over.

"All in black, probably covering a tragic haircut? Yeah, I see him," She confirmed.

"Dammit," I muttered, but I was relieved. Surely in a place as busy as this, there were bound to be some spirits.

"Can we at least wander over to somewhere to get lunch?" Nicki asked in desperation. Aura searching was not as much fun for her.

"Fine," I relented, mostly because I was getting a little hungry too. "Do you want to grab a snack or sit down somewhere?" I asked.

Nicki glanced at the time on her phone. "We've got time, let's find somewhere nice to sit and eat," She suggested. "Oh! How about that Spanish place down on Westmont Street? I fancy tapas," Nicki smiled and I laughed at her enthusiasm.

"Yes, ok fine," I smiled. It was the least I could do considering I was forcing her to go aura searching *and* borrowing her clothes once more tonight. We wandered past the busy weekend shoppers and got further out of the main shopping area. I still stared at people as they walked past, spinning my head to search for more people to look at, to sense their auras. Maybe I could just ask people to line up in an orderly fashion against a plain white wall?

"Is it this turning or the next?" Nicki asked as we walked down a residential street and I ran out of people to look at.

"The next one I think," I told her as we carried on walking.

"What's that?" Nicki asked as she ground to a halt. I followed her gaze. Smoke. I froze. No, not here, not now. I quickly bought my hands to my necklace. He wouldn't be able to see me.

"Em, I think that house is on fire!" Nicki shouted as she watched dark clouds of smoke billowing from a house ahead of us. My eyes narrowed, yes it was smoke, normal smoke from a fire. If Nicki could see it, then it wasn't the smoke spirit. Nicki broke into a sprint and I trailed after her. "What's happening?" Nicki asked as she reached the house, a woman stood on the pavement in front of it. The property was a detached Georgian home, looking large and grand – the smoke was coming out from round the rear.

"I've called the fire brigade and ambulances," The woman told us. "It's my neighbours, I don't even know if they're home or not," She told us. Nicki nodded and went to the grand wooden front door and tried the handle. The neighbour shook her head.

"I can't get in, the door is the same as mine, heavy thick wood, bolted on the inside. I've tried banging on the door and the windows, but the inside is filled with smoke." She told us.

"How many people live here?" Asked Nicki, her face filled with panic.

"Just three, a couple and their son," She told us.

"They could be stuck in there," I realised, the seriousness of the situation finally hitting me.

"We can't break the windows, the oxygen to the fire will only feed it, it could get bad," Nicki explained to me and the neighbour.

"I don't know what else to do," The neighbour said helplessly, tears springing to her eyes. "The woman on the phone told me to stand back and do nothing and wait for the fire engine to get here," She told us.

Nicki shook her head. "I know..." She started to say then shook her head again.

"Nicki, that house is filled with smoke, it looks worse at the back," I told myself more than anything. Who knew what was happening inside that house? On the outside you could almost mistake it as perfectly normal. Were the homeowner's actually home? Were they trapped inside? Already dead? I took a deep breath. "Nicki, I can help them," I told her, my voice wavering slightly.

Nicki's eyebrows furrowed. "What do you mean?" She asked.

"I can step into the Inbetween," I told her, lowering my voice. "I can go in there, via the Inbetween, and find out the situation, if there are people inside, if they're trapped, where they are so that that fire fighters can get to them as quickly as possible when they arrive," I told her. Realisation dawned on Nicki's face.

"But you barely know anything about this new power," Nicki frowned. "You only discovered that you go completely invisible when you go into the Inbetween, how do you know you will be able to hold it long enough? How do you know that you won't panic when you get in there, step of out the Inbetween and then be stuck inside a strangers house that is *on fire*?" She asked, incredulous.

I shook my head. "I don't," I told her and looked back towards the house. "But I know I have to try." I gave her arm a quick squeeze and darted off round the side of the large property. I found a secluded spot where I wouldn't be overlooked and placed my arms outstretched on the side of the building. I had no idea if this would work but all I knew was that I wanted it to work and me willing something to happen seemed the best and easiest way to make sure that it *did* happen.

I took a deep breath and closed my eyes. I thought about Christian and his ability to touch our world through the Inbetween and how strange it was to be able to do the same from the other side. Him wanting to step out of the Inbetween to touch our world and me wanting to step into the Inbetween to touch his.

I took a step forward, then another, feeling no resistance as I walked. I opened my eyes and took in my surroundings. My first thought was that I was in hell. That I had stepped too far into the Inbetween and out on the Other Side, straight into hell.

CHAPTER 21

The smoke was everywhere, thick and black. Safe in the Inbetween, I couldn't feel the heat of it on my skin or the lack of air in my lungs. *I'm safe.* I tried to hang onto the thought of Christian, and his life in the Inbetween. This was every day for him, except he couldn't go into people's homes – and I could.

I stepped further on into the house, I wasn't sure what room I was in, the smoke was too thick to see through. I was tempted to hold my breath and realised that I couldn't. There was no air in the Inbetween, I didn't need to breathe here. I decided to quicken my step as I walked through the walls of the room and into a large hallway. Or was it another room? There was no real way to tell. I looked around desperately. How much worse would it be for firefighters to find them if I couldn't? I moved quicker still, heading towards the back of the house. I gulped down my shock as I stepped into what I thought was the kitchen. It was completely ablaze. Fire, like I had never seen it before, devouring everything in its path. I wouldn't be able to tell if there were bodies here, the fire would have destroyed them completely. I turned quickly to go towards the front of the house, to find a staircase and look upstairs. For every moment that I hesitated, there were real live people who would be breathing in these fumes.

Towards the front of the house the smoke got thinner, less thick and black but still very present and threatening. I saw the staircase before I saw the people.

"You're alive," The woman said to me, in apparent shock. I turned to see her and a man, standing together near a door. They were clear to me, though the smoke should have made them hazy.

"You're dead," I said automatically and regretted it instantly. The couple had died in the fire, they were new spirits and the last thing they needed was someone stating the obvious truth.

"Please," The woman ran the few steps between us to get closer to me. "You must help us, we can't open the door," She said as she grabbed my hands in hers. My heart sunk. They didn't know they were dead.

"I'm so sorry," I whispered. "It's too late," My voice shook slightly.

"Not us," The man told me as he bent down near the floor. "Our son," He said, looking down.

On the floor, curled up tight, half leaning on the solid oak door, was a young boy, perhaps only three years old. He was shaking, mostly unconscious. The smoke was getting thicker now, faster, getting through gaps in the doors as the fire raged towards the front of the house.

"I... I can't touch things here," I told them shaking my head. I couldn't open the door in the Inbetween, but I could tell the firefighters to break down the door to get the kid out.

"Please, he doesn't have much time," the mother insisted, she went over to him and tried to stroke his head as her hand went straight through him.

Then I realised what I had to do. I had to step out of the Inbetween and into the house. I would have to unlock the door and get the child out. It might only take moments; the smoke may not even have to enter my lungs.

"I think I can do it," I told them looking at the door, mostly covered by smoke. "How does it open?" I asked.

"There is a deadbolt, here, at the bottom and one on the top. Pull them both to the left and then pull down the handle," The father instructed me. I nodded.

My body shook as I closed my eyes and tried to concentrate. I had never had to try and leave the Inbetween before, it just happened, naturally. I imagined in my head what it would be like to be back in my world, to feel the heat of the smoke, the black clouds trying to force their way into my lungs. For a moment I wasn't sure whether I was really feeling it or imagining it, but as the warmth on my skin startled me, I took a sharp breath inward, and my lungs filled with smoke. Coughing automatically, I opened my eyes and quickly fell to the ground. Using my cardigan to cover my mouth I crawled closer to the boy on the floor.

"I'm here to help," I managed to splutter out to him. His eyes flickered but there was no other movement. I had to get him out of here, and fast. I felt for the bottom of the door and touched the warm metal of the deadlock. I slid it across quickly and it went across easily with a satisfying thud. As I stood, I realised I would need to move the child if I had to open to the door. I let my cardigan fall from around my mouth and felt my lungs protest as I held my breath. I scooped the boy up in my arms and my head spun to the hallway door as colour caught my eye. The flames were creeping through, devouring the door, and getting closer, bringing a wave of new black thick clouds of smoke with it. Frantically I shifted the boy in my arms as his head flopped against my shoulder. I lifted an arm up to the door, searching for the second bolt. I found it and pulled with all my might. It wasn't as easy as the first one, but it gave way to my insistent pull and unlocked. Then after a frantic pull on the handle, the door was open, and the smoke escaped with us.

I sucked in fresh air, it seemed to fill my lungs with a burning sensation causing me to cough harder. I stumbled down the front porch steps with the boy still in my arms. Nicki and the neighbour came rushing over as I lay the boy on the grass at the front of the house.

"CPR," I coughed out, pointing at the boy, but Nicki was way ahead of me. Checking his airways, Nicki had already started. I coughed and spluttered as I sat down. If I felt this bad after just a few seconds in there, how would this boy be feeling? I looked around to find the spirits of his parents but they were nowhere to be seen.

After a moment, I heard the boy coughing and spluttering, his little lungs wheezing, but very much alive. Nicki was crying with joy. Then I heard the sirens.

"Oh, thank goodness," The neighbour said as she looked down the road then back towards me. "How did you get in there?" She asked. "I thought I had checked everything," She questioned, confused. I shrugged and shook my head and held my throat like it was difficult to talk. "You saved his life," She told me then looked at Nicki. "You both did." Her eyes went back to the house, smoke still pouring out the door and the fire now licking at the roof of the property. "His parents?..." She started to ask but then saw the look in my eyes. I shook my head solemnly. She nodded, understanding. The boy coughed again and the neighbour bent down to him, cradling him in her arms. I grabbed at Nicki as I saw the fire engine pull down the road.

"We have to go," I staged whispered to her.

"What? No. You need to be checked out by the ambulance," She told me.

"I'm fine," I insisted sternly. "But we have to go, right *now*." I told her and pulled at her arm, but Nicki pulled back. "I have just got the journalists off my back, how many do you think will be camping out on my front lawn come the morning once they discover that the 'beacon of hope' pulled out a boy from a burning building?" I asked her quickly, the fire engine pulled up outside the house and firefighters started pouring out of it. With a flash of regret in her eyes Nicki nodded and together we ran down the road, our disappearance unnoticed in the firefighters attempt to battle the fire raging through the house.

*

Safe back at home, lunch had been forgotten about while we recovered in my room, only half-heartedly looking at clothes.

"It's already online," Nicki told me, scrolling through her phone.

"What does it say?" I asked, desperate to know that the little boy was ok. Nicki scanned through the page on her phone.

"They think the fire started in the morning, the parents dying from smoke inhalation while they slept. The boy was in the lounge watching tv when he saw the smoke and went to the front door as he had been taught, but he couldn't get the door open. A passing stranger managed to climb into the house and save the little boy, while another performed CPR. There is no further information on these people at this time. The little boy is currently in a stable condition, expected to make a full recovery due to the acts of these strangers." She read aloud. I let out a long breath.

"I'm glad he's going to be ok." I said, thinking of the parents that he would now have to grow up without. At least he would grow up.

"Did you see his parents?" Nicki asked. I nodded.

"They knew that it was too late for them, they asked me to save their son," a lump came to my throat.

"It was very brave of you, having to step out of the Inbetween to get him and open the door," Nicki told me quietly.

"I think the firefighters would have reached him in time," I told her, not sure whether I had really made a difference. Nicki shook her head.

"I'm not so sure," She told me and fiddled with the edge of a top that was slung across the bed. She sighed. "We saved his life and no one will ever know," She told me, a look of regret in her eyes.

"Trust me, it's much better to do an act of kindness and have no one thank you for it. A truer kind of goodness." I told her.

She shrugged. "I guess, but unlike you, I don't mind being on the news," She laughed, I gave her a half smile. "So… when you saw the parents…" She started to say and hesitated for a moment. "Did you see their auras?" She asked.

"Dammit," I cursed as I realised, I hadn't seen anything at all.

CHAPTER 22

As Nicki and I tried to get today's events out of our heads and I ended up having two showers to get the smoke smell out of my hair, I began to look forward to the normalness that an evening with Jack would entail.

Nicki left and Jack turned up at my house right on time, as expected. I had convinced mum to go out for the night, only feeling a touch of guilt about making her leave her own house.

Jack came bearing food. "I didn't know what you might fancy, so I got a little of everything," He grinned, holding up takeaway bags. I couldn't help but laugh as we spread the food out on the coffee table, he really had got a bit of everything. "Here, try dipping your pizza into this curry, tastes better than I thought it would," He laughed as I pulled a face. We'd put a film on but neither of us were really watching it.

"I may go into a food coma," I smiled at him, thankful for my choice of a floaty top that might cover any carb bloating and I bit into another mozzarella stick. "You must let me give you some money for this, it must have cost a bomb," I told him.

"Don't be silly, it's on me." He shook his head, wiping crumbs from his lips.

"No, I'm going to have to insist this time, it's not even like you have a job..." I paused. "Oh man! I can't believe I forgot to ask you! How did the job interview go?" I asked, smacking my head, feeling too self-involved.

Jack laughed. "I got the job, so don't worry, I can afford the food." He told me with a playful smile.

"Oh, Jack that's amazing! I'm so happy for you!" I put the slice of pizza down and leant over to give him a quick hug.

"Well, before you go getting all amorous, I did come over here with an ulterior motive," The smile slipped from his face. "I need to ask a favour," He said quietly. I raised an eyebrow.

"Well that's two meals you've bought me now so I figure I could probably stretch to one favour," I said, trying to ease the tension. What could he possibly want?

"I feel bad asking, after everything that went down last time, and I completely understand if you say no. I didn't come here tonight wanting it, it was only after you said yes that I thought maybe I could ask…" He said quickly and stopped.

"Oh come on Jack, you're killing me here," I laughed, trying to get him to lighten up a little, but the curiosity really was killing me.

"Do you remember when we were fifteen and I missed those last few weeks of school?" He asked.

I nodded. "Yeah I remember, you had lost your uncle and you were struggling with it," I remembered. Then I realised what he was going to ask. "Oh…. Oh Jack…" I started to say but wasn't sure how to finish the sentence.

"Like I said, you can say no, it's no big deal, I don't even expect you to say yes, not after the way I behaved. And I don't want you to think it's some kind of test, I really do believe you," He started speaking quickly again, I leant over and put my hand on his to reassure him.

"I don't think that," I told him calmly. "But you have to understand, I'm still new at this and I've only tried calling someone once. Nicki's Grams was an accident," I took a deep breath. "But I can try," I finished. I watched as tears sprung to his eyes.

"I never got to say a proper goodbye," He whispered, trying to keep control of his voice.

"I would need something of his, something personal," I told him.

Jack nodded and reached inside his jacket pocket and pulled out a tie.

"I thought as much. This was his lucky tie, he used to wear it on first dates and told me he'd always get the girl, as long as he was wearing this. Dad let me keep it after he died," He smiled sadly, fingering the silver tie in-between his fingers. I reached over for the tie and almost reluctantly, he handed it over. I tried to decide if I could feel some kind of presence in the tie, some kind of connection, but I wasn't sure. It would be nice to learn how to hone my skills so that I could do more than just see. I wanted to feel as well, just like Angela could.

"We'll have to do it outside," I told Jack as I stood up and grabbed my hoodie. "He won't be allowed in here," I told him. I wondered about Christian, whether he would be out there, or still off somewhere sulking. Hoping he would be sensitive enough to keep his distance, I led Jack to the backdoor.

There was no sign of Christian as we walked out and made our way to the patio table to take a seat. Jack looked more solemn than I'd ever seen him. I looked down at the tie for a moment. "I can't promise you that this will work," I warned Jack, not confident in my own abilities. I'd spent so much time practising how to disappear I hadn't yet thought about spending more time on calling other spirits. For one thing, I didn't have anyone to call. Maybe this would be good practise at the very least.

"It's fine, the fact that you're willing to give it a try, even after how I behaved, that means a lot to me," Jack said sincerely. I took a deep breath.

"What was your uncle's name, Jack?" I asked.

"Ben," He told me.

I took another deep breath and closed my eyes. I gripped the tie tightly, feeling the smoothness against my skin. "Ben," I called out. "My name is Emily, I'm here with your nephew, Jack. We would love it if you could come by and speak to us," I said aloud, feeling a little foolish. It hadn't seemed so silly with Angela. I waited a moment and opened my eyes, but it was only me and Jack sitting in my garden. I closed my eyes again. "Ben, don't be scared, I am a friend of Jack's and he would really like the chance to speak to you, he never got the chance to say goodbye to you, please give him that chance back today," I asked, raising my voice a little. How loud did a person have to be, to be heard on the Other Side? I gripped the tie tighter and willed Ben to my side. I wish I knew what he looked like.

"I'm here Emily," A voice said gently, I jumped, fairly sure I was never going to get used to this. I opened my eyes to see a man standing next to Jack, he seemed only a few years older than us.

"Ben?" I asked and he nodded.

"He's here?" Jack asked, his voice filled with awe.

"I think so," I said and smiled. "He's tall," I described. "Perhaps just as tall as you. Darker than you though, but you have the same chin." I told him.

"We call it the Gilbert chin," Ben grinned and at that point I knew without a doubt that they were related.

"He says you call it the Gilbert chin," I told Jack, smiling, Ben's grin was infectious.

The noise that came from Jack was half gasp and half laugh.

"It's really him," Jack whispered. "Quick, ask him what the last thing was that he said to me?" Jack asked, leaning forward.

"He can hear you," I laughed and looked up at Ben. Ben brought his hand to his chin and tapped it as if pondering.

"I told him he sucked at football and should take up synchronised swimming instead," Ben laughed and I repeated for Jack. Jack almost fell about with laughter.

"This is amazing," Jack leant over and gave my hand a squeeze. "Thank you," He said. Ben raised an eyebrow.

"Hey, hello? I'm here all the way from the afterlife, thank you very much," He teased and again I repeated to Jack in-between giggles. This really was amazing.

"Ben, I just wanted to say thank you, for everything you did for me when I was younger, for being like a brother to me. We were all heartbroken when you… left. I never got the chance to say goodbye and I never thought I would have this chance now. I just want to tell you that I love you and I miss you every day. I never thought…" Jack paused as tears rolled down his cheeks and he had to take a deep breath. I wasn't sure if spirits could cry, but if they could, they would look something like Ben, whose face was filled with sorrow. He leant down, close to Jack and for a moment I wished I could transfer every power that I had so that Jack could reach out and hug him.

"It sucks that it happened, but it doesn't matter to me that we never said goodbye, because I know that you love me, and I love you too. You will always be the son that I never had. But I'm at peace here, I check in on you and I know that you're doing ok, and I'm so proud of you." Ben said to Jack, I repeated to Jack as tears sprung to my eyes. For a moment, Jack just clung onto my hand as he tried to compose himself. "I'm going to see you again Jack," Ben continued. "When you're old and grey and your time is up. But before then I'm going to watch you finish growing up, I'm going to watch you get married and I'm going to watch you attempt parenthood, then I'm going to watch over those kids as if they were my own grandchildren. Then one day you'll be at peace too and we'll watch over them together," Ben confirmed, he reached out for Jack's shoulder, but Jack didn't seem to notice as his fingers went through him. I repeated for Jack and gave him a small smile.

"He doesn't have much longer," I warned Jack gently. Jack gave a small nod and took a deep breath.

"You know, I got better at football," Jack attempted a feeble smile.

"No, you didn't," Ben laughed, and Jack laughed too once I repeated. "Thank you, Emily," Ben said directly to me and gave me a smile. "Look after him, he's one of the good ones you know," He smiled.

"I know," I said and smiled back. "Goodbye Ben," I said.

"Goodbye Ben," Jack repeated.

"Goodbye," Ben smiled sadly and faded away.

Jack and I sat in silence for a moment. Tears trickled down Jack's face, but he had a faint smile as well. "You ok?" I asked quietly as I gave his hand a squeeze.

"Best second date ever," He told me with a small smile.

CHAPTER 23

The next morning, I was awake before Mum so took the chance to make her breakfast for a change. I brought her up a bacon sandwich and an orange juice and knocked on her bedroom door with my elbow. I heard a groan and took that as a 'come in'. I perched on the bottom of her bed.

"Breakfast," I declared, waving the sandwich underneath her nose. Mum rolled over and pulled the covers over her head. "Oh dear," I said. "Hungover?"

"Your fault," I heard her mutter underneath the covers. I stifled a laugh.

"Ok, I'm going to leave these here. For whenever you're ready," I smiled and left the plate and glass on her bedside table.

I'd wanted the chance to talk to her properly, but she was in no state. Yesterday was the first time that I'd actually been in bed before for my mum. I was glad that she'd had a good night out, but after the success of calling Ben for Jack, and how much that meant to him, I realised that I wanted to do this more. I wanted to be able to help people, whether that was giving them the chance to say the goodbye that they never had, or whether it would be helping people move onto the Other Side. Either way, none of these things could go much more forward without telling my mum the truth. Plus, I was in a different situation now. I didn't just have to tell her and then hope for the best that she wouldn't think I was too crazy. I could prove it now, I could call on someone, maybe a grandparent of hers, or just disappear completely. She may have a heart attack, and no one would ever fully accept it as quickly and easily as Nicki had, but she would come around to the whole idea. I was confident in that.

Just making the decision to tell mum felt like a weight off my shoulders. Probably best not to be done when she was hungover, but soon. I went back downstairs feeling lighter as I opened the backdoor to call for Christian. He was already outside and visible. Sitting at the patio table where Jack had sat last night. He didn't look up as I walked over. I decided to ignore his sulking.

"You'll never guess what I did last night," I smiled, refusing to let him spoil my good mood. "I summoned a spirit for Jack. It was his uncle; they were always really close, and he never got the chance to say goodbye to him." I sat down at the table. "It was so lovely being able to reunite them, so moving and touching," I said as Christian looked solemnly at the table.

"Sounds like the best second date ever," Christian grumbled, and I froze. He had been here then, seen it all.

"Well, I don't know about that," I said, deciding to ignore it. "But I think I'm getting better at this whole spirit thing; I think it's getting easier. I mean, I know I have a lot more to learn but for once I think it's manageable and actually, I *want* to manage it. Feels like a huge breakthrough for me," I finished and smiled.

Christian swung round to look at me in the eye. "Do you think that this is funny?" He said, his nostrils flared with anger. "Is this a game to you?" He asked.

I shook my head "What do you mean?" I asked quietly and he quickly simmered down, looking like he regretted his outburst.

"Kissing me one moment, then inviting other men over the next? I am from a completely different century Emily, but time has not changed all that much, in my world that was considered bad form and I believe it still is today." He folded his arms and looked away from me, like a petulant child.

"No, ok Christian, you're right. That isn't acceptable and I apologise for allowing Jack over here, I knew that it would upset you, but it was not my intention to hurt you. I told you the other day, that kiss should never have happened. It was wonderful and I don't regret it, but you and I can't do things like that," I told him sadly. Sadness flashed in his eyes as he uncrossed his arms and leant towards me.

"You cannot deny that we have a connection here," He told me curtly.

"I'm not denying anything Christian, what I'm trying to tell you is what you already know, you just don't want to hear it. You're a spirit, and I'm not, I might have a foot in your world but I'm not there and I don't plan to be for a very long time. Whatever this is, between us, we can't let it get too far, if we slip up again then this friendship has to end, and I don't want that," I told him. Every word I said seemed to sting him like I was slashing him with knives.

"So, that is it? All feelings towards me ignored and pushed aside. You're going to choose Jack just because he is alive?" He asked.

"I'm not *choosing* anyone," I told him. "This isn't some sort of competition here. You know what I'm going through at the moment Christian, I don't have time for anything romantic here. I need you in my life, and I don't want to lose you, but I also don't want this to get messy and complicated. Not with you and not with Jack. I'm not choosing anyone. I'm choosing to be alone." I told him sternly, this conversation seemed bizarre to me. As if I could really be arguing with him about this. "Just a few weeks ago I was lying in a pool of my own blood, willing myself to believe that I was dead," I said in a small voice. "Every night I go to sleep and I dream of a sea of screaming faces dying around. Every time I try to save them, I try something different and nothing ever works. No one lives. And every morning I wake up and remember that it's not just a dream, it's a reality. *My* reality... and you think I'm interested in choosing a man to spend time with?" I asked, almost disgusted in him. How quickly they can all forget, where I never will.

Christian stared at the table for a moment. I couldn't tell by his face what he was thinking. "If I were alive," Christian said slowly. "Would you choose me then?" He asked, a flash of annoyance crossed my face. I watched as his face fell and for a moment, my heart ached for him, he looked so lost, so rejected.

"It doesn't matter," I told him curtly.

"Just suppose for a minute that I was alive as Jack. If I were still me, alive and well, beating heart and had the ability to step inside your house. Just imagine it for a moment, indulge me," He asked. "If I were here with you, alive and well, supporting you, helping you, trusting you, loving you, if I were doing all this with flesh and bone, would you choose me then? Would you want to be with me?" He searched my eyes desperately and I was lost for words. If I was really honest with myself, would I want to be with Christian if he were alive? I mean, really, it was impossible to tell. If he were alive maybe we would have never met, but if by some chance he was alive and he'd helped me the way that he had, supported me and cared for me, made me laugh when I was sad, helped me take control when I was scared...

"Yes," I told him. "But this is torture for both of us. The best thing we can possibly do now is just put these feelings aside, realise that it's impossible and try and find a way to move forward." I vaguely remembered my mum saying something similar when I was younger about moving on from my dad.

"What if we could do it though?" Christian leaned closer and took my hand in his. "What if we could find a way to bring me back? So that we could be together?" He asked seriously, staring into my eyes.

"It's impossible," I told him and paused. "Isn't it?" I asked carefully.

"Emily, you have done things these last few weeks that most people would call a miracle. You have managed things that people have cast aside as impossible. Do you really want to look me in the eye and tell me right now that you are absolutely sure that this would be impossible?" He asked, his grip tightening on my hand. I took a deep breath, not wanting to admit that he was right, that it could be possible, but not wanting to raise his hopes. I got up off my chair, shaking his hand loose.

"I wouldn't even know where to start," I whispered, this wasn't walking through walls or reuniting lost loved ones. This was raising the dead for goodness sake and every part of the conversation felt *wrong*.

"I think I have an idea; I have got some spirits I need to talk to first, I just need to know that you could be open minded about this. That you believe in me enough to *try*." He asked.

I swallowed down my revulsion. This was not something I wanted to try, even for Christian's sake. I saw mum in the corner of my eye come into the kitchen and pour herself a coffee. "I have to go Christian, my mum is here," I said and turned to leave.

"No wait!" He called and grabbed my wrist, he pulled me to him so sharply I actually felt myself being torn from my world into the Inbetween. He became so much brighter here, so much more real and alive. He held his hands on my waist, pulling me to him. "Look me at, feel me. Alive to you and real." He whispered. "Imagine this, every day. Walking down the street holding hands, getting to go on dates and out for meals. Me, getting to live the life that I was robbed off. Getting to grow old, get married, have children. With you, if that's what you want." His amber eyes stared down at me whilst I was locked in his embrace. He had missed out on so much life, but whether I could be a ticket back for him, I wasn't sure. There would be rules involved, surely. Didn't life always require a balance? I was certain I wouldn't be able to do it, and sure that I didn't want to. But maybe he needed me to try, or to look like I was willing to try at least. Maybe he just needed someone on his side.

"I will try for you," I told him. He held me in the Inbetween for a moment longer, searching my eyes for the answers that he so desperately wanted to hear. Slowly, he nodded and let go of me. I turned and opened the back door and stepped into the kitchen.

I let out a long sigh of relief. I was going to have to do something about this.

"That is the last time I try keeping up with the younger girls from the office," Mum groaned as she stepped back into the kitchen, cradling her cup of coffee. "Please tell me your date was worth it?" She laughed.

I flashed her a smile. "I think it probably was, yeah," I told her, thinking of Jack's face when he realised I was talking to his Uncle. "Mum, when you're a little more alive, is there any chance that I could get a lift to Nicki's?" I asked her.

Mum swallowed the last dregs of her coffee and nodded. "One of these days you need to learn to drive," She told me.

"Driving would have been a waste in London," I told her for about the millionth time in two years.

"So, you're going back there?" She asked curiously. I paused.

"No idea," I smiled innocently.

"Hey, did you see this?" Mum asked, scrolling through her phone.

"What's that?" I asked, reaching for the orange juice.

"There was a fire at a house just down the road, near the shopping centre," Mum read from her phone and for a moment my heart started beating faster. Nothing to worry about, no danger here, I tried to tell myself.

"Oh yeah, I read about that, apparently only the child survived," I told her sadly. I had thought about going back there, to reach out to his parents somehow, to check that they had found peace, but I couldn't risk the neighbour recognising me.

"Yeah but that's not the strange part, apparently some passing strangers managed to break into the house to save him and were gone before the police arrived. Looks like they appeared, rescued the boy and disappeared just as quick. The little boy who was saved has been quoted saying that an Angel saved him, isn't that lovely?" Mum smiled as she scrolled through the rest of the article on her phone. I thought back to only yesterday when I forced myself to step out of the Inbetween to a smoke-filled room and scooped the boy into my arms. I seemingly appeared from nowhere, but I had been fairly sure that he had been unconscious. A lump gathered in my throat.

"That's sweet," I murmured. "Now, go get dressed," I ushered her out of the room to go up the stairs and get ready before she could read any more.

*

"That's a pretty necklace," Mum told me as she grabbed her car keys. I'd put on the necklace Angela had given me.

"Thanks, it was from a friend," I smiled as we got into the car.

"Tigers Eye, right?" Mum asked as she started up the car. I blinked.

"That's right…" I said. Mum laughed.

"You don't have to look so surprised, there are some things that I know. I used to be really into crystals when I was younger, all their different properties, I thought they were fascinating." She said,

"Really?" I asked, perhaps mum would be more open to the unexplained than I'd given her credit for. "Do you know what Tiger's Eye is for?" I asked.

Mum thought for a moment and a touch of sadness reached her eyes as she realised. "Protection," She confirmed sadly. I nodded.

"That's impressive," I told her.

"Not really," She shrugged. "There are a lot of crystals that all look similar, a whole range of blue ones and green ones that I always struggled to tell apart. Tiger's Eye was always quite distinctive."

"Well, what did you use crystals for?" I asked, wondering if she had ever felt the need to wear a Tiger's Eye around her neck.

She smiled warmly. "I used to sleep with a huge chunk of rose quartz under my pillow, hoping it would bring me love," She laughed, remembering fondly.

"Oh yeah?" I said. "And how did that work out?" I asked.

"Well, I met your father shortly afterwards," She laughed.

"Ah, not so well then," I laughed too.

"Ah, I wouldn't say that," Mum flashed her eyes towards me. "Then I had you, and to me, there is no purer love in the world," Mum said fondly.

"Soppy git," I teased but turned my head so I wouldn't let her see the tears that had sprung to my eyes. I definitely needed to tell her everything.

CHAPTER 24

Nicki was surprised when she opened her door, I hadn't called ahead to warn her. "Was the date that good you needed to tell me in person?" She laughed as she led me into the kitchen.

"It was good, but not for the reasons you might think," I told her. She was wide-eyed as I explained what happened with Jack and his uncle. I attempted to describe the raw emotion of the experience, but it was difficult to put into words.

"Oh Em, that must have meant so much to him," Nicki said in hushed tones.

"Yeah I think it did, but that wasn't the reason I came over," I told her, and she raised her eyebrows in curiosity. "I need to talk to your Grams again," I said.

"Ok..." She answered and looked around. "Is she... here?" She asked. I shook my head.

"I think it was just a fluke last time, I think I will need to call her." I said.

"Ok, any particular reason?" She queried. I hesitated. Most of mine and Christian's conversations I had kept to myself. Mostly to avoid a telling off from Nicki about getting too close to him but also because it felt private, everything that we had shared and experienced together.

"Christian said some things today... I just need to check it with someone I can trust." I told her. Nicki tapped her nails on the kitchen counter and looked at me, expecting more. "I'll explain it all, I promise, I just need to check with your Grams first." I told her, just hoping she would trust me.

"Ok fine," She sighed. "It's not like you really need my permission anyway," She rolled her eyes.

"Well, I kind of need something personal of hers, something that I can use to connect with her. Otherwise I'm just going to have to hang around your house every day hoping that she pops up," I laughed. Nicki thought about it for a moment.

"Oh!" She exclaimed and ran out of the room and up the stairs. I followed her. By the time I caught up with her, she was in her parents' room, rummaging through her mum's vanity table.

"Are your parents' home?" I asked worriedly, not wanting to get caught. Nicki shook her head.

"Dad had to go into work and mum is out doing the weekly shop. I'm not sure how much time we'll have though," She said as she opened another drawer. "Here it is," She declared, holding up a silver necklace with a small cross on it. She brought it over to me. "It was Grams, she used to wear it every day. Mum worries about losing it so never wears it. Do you think this would work?" Nicki asked.

"I'm sure it will," I smiled, taking the necklace from her. Again, I hoped to feel something when I touched it. Some kind of warmth or connection, but it was just a necklace. "Shall we go to your room?" I asked and Nicki nodded and led the way.

Her room was even messier than usual, I raised my eyebrows but said nothing.

"This is your fault," Nicki laughed. "I was finding clothes for your date," She smirked as she kicked a pile of clothes out of the way. I decided to perch on her bed, which was unmade but at least I was fairly sure no spiders would crawl out from underneath it. I slipped my necklace off from around my throat and let it sit on the bed next to me.

I took a deep breath and closed my eyes as Nicki sat on the other side of the bed, "Grams, it's Emily. I really need to talk to you, I need your help, please come to talk to me," I asked quietly, half afraid that Nicki's mum might come home any second. I waited a moment and opened my eyes and quickly scanned the room. I repeated what I said slowly and a little more loudly. I opened my eyes again and watched as Nicki nervously fiddled with the edge of her duvet. I waited another moment and then slowly, Grams came into view, smiling at us both.

"It's nice to see you again Emily," She smiled, and I was surprised to notice the necklace that she wore around her neck, exactly identical to the one I was holding.

"Thank you for coming Grams, I'm sorry to have to bother you," I told her.

"It's no bother. I was surprised to hear from you, looks like you've come quite a way in a short time," She smiled.

"I have," I nodded. "It's mostly down to a spirit friend I made, he's been helping me," I told her, watching her expression cautiously. "He's stuck here, in the Inbetween, he never crossed over." I explained, she nodded solemnly.

"You need to be wary of those in the Inbetween Emily," Grams told me. "If they fear what will happen when they cross over, you can't know that they led a good life in your world." She said,

"No, I know why he stayed here, and I understand it. What I'm worried about..." I hesitated as I glanced over at Nicki, who was openly watching my one-sided conversation with a mixture of amusement and awe. "I'm worried because he has got a little attached to me. He's talking about wanting to live again and that I might be able to help him do that," I told her. Both Nicki and Grams frowned with an expression that was so similar to each other's that I almost laughed.

"Emily, that is not possible," Grams told me, shaking her head.

"No, I don't think it is, but he seems fairly sure that there might be a way," I told her.

"Emily," Grams paused, uncertain. "When you look at me now, you see an image of the person that my mind remembers. I am made up of a trick of the light, a trick that your brain tells you is a person, but I'm not. My body was buried, I am not made up of skin and bone, no matter what I look like to you. I am a soul, a spirit, an energy. Just like he is. My image is the form of what I resembled in life, but there is no way to make this solid. My spirit may live on after death, but you cannot reconstruct my body to enable me to live again. It is the same for him. Our bodies failed us on earth, we cannot go back there," She confirmed. A part of me felt relieved, but mostly I just felt sad. Christian's hopes would be dashed, and it would be me who would have to tell him. "How long has your spirit friend been in the Inbetween?" Grams asked.

"Over 100 years," I told her. She nodded slowly.

"You need to be wary," Grams warned me again. "A spirit that has been that alone, stuck in the Inbetween for that long... He will be lost, and lonely. You must try not to let him get too attached to you." She said. I chewed on my bottom lip as I considered this.

"Grams... Do you know if someone killed someone in life, but in self-defence, trying to save someone... would they still find peace on the Other Side?" I asked. Grams looked at me sadly.

"I'm afraid that I do not know," She answered. I didn't think she would. I'd like to think if I told Christian that I could help him pass over to the other side then maybe he wouldn't need to hold onto hope that he could live again. Instead, maybe he would be glad that he would find peace. But he had still killed someone, and though he had stayed around to watch over his sister, maybe a small part of him was also afraid of what might be waiting for him on the Other Side. If indeed there was a bad part of the Other Side that no one seemed to come back from. Could I bear sending him to the Other Side not knowing if he would find peace or not?

"Thank you, Grams," I said sadly, and without hesitation I took a deep breath and reached out for her, in the Inbetween, to embrace her. I received gasps from both Nicki and Grams as I disappeared out of Nicki's sight and held Gram's solid form.

"How can you…" Grams started to say then stopped and hugged me back. She then held onto my shoulders and took a step back and examined me. "You can see and touch the Inbetween," She stated in shock. I nodded. Grams shook her head. "I can feel him on you, this spirit." She said slowly. "His energy is all over you," She shook her head again. "You need to take a step back from him Emily," She warned again. "This will not be good for either of you, he will get lost in you and you will get lost in the Inbetween. If you need to do this, to carry on with this, you cannot let yourself get attached to a spirit. We do not belong in this world Emily, any more than you belong in ours. To merge the worlds together like this… it's not right. It creates an imbalance. Fleeting moments like ours can be manageable but you are connecting with this spirit for so long… It's dangerous Emily," Grams warned sternly. I nodded but I wasn't sure what it all meant. I took a step back from her, away from the Inbetween, appearing back into Nicki's view. She jumped again as I reappeared. "I have to go," Grams said sadly and looked towards Nicki. "Tell her to tidy this room," She scolded gently, with a small smile on her face, as she faded away.

After a moment, Nicki leant over to me. "So, what was that all about?" She asked curiously.

I shrugged. "Grams said to tidy your room," I tried to laugh but Nicki looked serious.

"Does Christian want to live again?" She asked. I tried to avoid her gaze.

"I think it's more complicated than that, but he seems to think there might be a way. Grams has confirmed it though, there is nothing we can do," I said sadly.

"Well of course not!" Nicki exclaimed. "You can't bring a spirit back to life!" She almost yelled.

"I know!" I told her. "I wasn't planning on it anyway, I just needed to make sure that it really wasn't possible, before Christian comes up with some insane plan to even try it." I told her.

"This is bad, isn't it," Nicki stated. "He's become too reliant on you, got it into his head that you can help him," Nicki continued fiddling with the edge of her duvet. "How is he going to react when you tell him you can't?" She asked and I shook my head. I had no idea.

"I think I might be able to help him cross over," I decided to tell Nicki. "But first I need to know for sure if he's going to find peace or not. He deserves that much at least." I told her.

"How in the world are you going to know that?" She asked.

"I don't know... I know that he killed someone, protecting his little sister... I mean, it's manslaughter at best, but do you think that would mean he wouldn't find peace?" I asked. Nicki shrugged.

"Could you find out more about what happened? If you knew the details you might be able to get some clarity on how exactly it went down," She suggested.

"I know that he didn't mean to kill him, he tackled him, to get his sister out of the man's hands, I don't think he meant to hurt him," I told her. Who knows what was going through his head at the time? Who knows how well he could remember it, after all these years? Nicki leant back on her headrest and closed her eyes. I went over to her table and placed down her Gram's necklace. Then reached for my necklace on her bed and secured it back around my throat.

"Do you remember," Nicki began. "When we were at school and we had to do a project about World War One?" Nicki asked. I shrugged half-heartedly. I didn't really remember. "Remember how everyone just went onto Google and we thought we would be clever by getting information from actual books so our project wouldn't be the same as everyone else's?" She asked.

"Yeah sort of, what's your point?" I asked.

"Well, the librarian showed us all these archives of old newspapers, we managed to get stories of what was happening during the time, in each town, giving our project a much deeper level than anyone else's," She reminded me. I did remember, and I remembered doing quite well on the project. I realised where she was going with this.

"You think they'll be a newspaper story on Christian's death?" I asked.

"Well think about it, a girl gets half kidnapped, brother is dubbed a tragic hero in saving her before his death. That had to have made the news. If we can find out more information about what happened, from other people's point of view, we'd have a much firmer grasp of what happened and whether he's headed for peace or not," She told me.

"Yeah but even if the newspaper does call him a hero and praises him for his actions, that's just one journalist's opinion, can that really be relied upon to tell the fate of what will happen to him on the Other Side?" I asked. I wondered whether there was some mystical man in the sky ticking off a list deciding who got to end up where.

"Emily, what if Christian didn't kill anyone? What if he only thought he had? He died before he really found out, what if he just knocked the guy unconscious and assumed that he was dead?" Nicki asked excitedly. It's something I hadn't considered. Surely if they had both died then they would have seen each other in the Inbetween as the other guy wouldn't have crossed over, and Christian had never mentioned seeing him.

"You might be onto something," I said excitedly. "To the library!" I cheered as Nicki got off the bed.

*

The library was quiet for a Sunday. We had had to wait until Nicki's mum came home so we could borrow the car. I wasn't quite sure if she believed us that we were going to the library, but she had let us use the car.

"Ok, on here you can tap into the British Library which holds all the archives for newspapers in the UK, up until the 1700s. Do you know what year you're looking for?" The librarian asked. I looked blankly at Nicki. I hadn't thought of this.

"Ok, so he was 24 when it happened," I told Nicki. "And he was born in..." I struggled to remember. "1850?" I wondered aloud. "Around then," I shrugged. Nicki sighed.

"Can we search for everything in 1873 to 1875 please?" She asked.

"Yes, no problem, the search function is up here, so select the dates from the drop down here..." Nicki clicked as the women showed her what to do.

"There are over 100,000 newspapers here," Nicki stated, open mouthed.

"Seriously?" I groaned. "This is going to take forever." I leant back in my chair.

"Erm, you can filter it further." The librarian suggested. "Is there a particular newspaper you're looking for?" The librarian asked.

"No," I said. "Oh, but we're probably looking for an Oxford newspaper?" I asked.

"That helps," Smiled the librarian. "You can filter by county over here, look," She said pointing at the screen. Nicki filtered on Oxfordshire.

"Less than 2000 hits," Nicki said, relieved.

"Ok, I'll do the same on this computer, if I start page one and you start on the last page and we make our way into the middle, we should be able to cover everything." I told Nicki and we got the work, thanking the Librarian.

We quickly discovered that even with lessening it to 2000 hits, the task was extremely tedious. The problem with old newspapers was that there were no big flashy headlines with pictures like there was now. Every story seemed to join to the next one and it was just sentence after sentence, trying to scan the page to find the word murder or even attempting to find Christian's name was near on impossible.

After two hours of searching, Nicki leant back in her chair and rubbed the back of her neck. "Ok maybe this was a bad idea," She moaned as she stretched her arms up above her head. "It's been two hours and I'm only in May. Can't we just ask Christian for the exact date at the very least?" She asked.

"I don't think he'd be too pleased with the fact that I told you, and I can't very well explain to him why we're doing it," I told her as I clicked onto the next page.

"Surely he'd want to help?" She queried.

"Right now, Christian is set on coming back to life, not crossing over. I think if I can convince him that he will find peace, then I might talk him round to at least trying. No point raising his hopes if we can't find anything," I told her, scanning through the words on the page on the screen.

Nicki sighed again, loudly, but returned to the computer and clicked onto the next page. Not long afterwards, Nicki spoke. "I think I've found something," She whispered. "What was Christian's last name?" She asked. I looked up from my screen.

"Shit, I don't know," I told her. How could I not know? "What does it say?" I asked.

"The Turner residence was broken into by two young men… blah blah blah… attempted abduction!" Nicki almost squealed. I rolled my chair over to her and tried to get a closer look.

"Turner family are in mourning after the loss of their beloved son…" Nicki carried on reading.

"Does it say anything about the men that broke in? Did one die?"

"Hang on," Nicki muttered as she scanned the screen, getting closer. "One man escaped and is still being sought after. The second man… was killed at the scene." Nicki finished.

"Oh," I said sadly. I knew it was a long shot, but I couldn't help but hope. This brought me back to square one. Not able to bring Christian back but hardly able to help him move on either. Would he be stuck in the Inbetween forever? Would I?

"Henry Turner… named after his father." Nicki continued to read. "Henry?" She queried as she leant closer to the computer screen.

"Whose Henry?" I asked, not really caring at this point.

"I'm not sure…" Nicki muttered as her eyes scanned the screen. "Oh," She hesitated. "Henry is the name of the brother that died saving his sister." Nicki shot me a quizzical look. "Did Christian not tell you his real name?" She asked. My eyebrows furrowed.

"Why would he make up a name?" I wondered aloud as Nicki's attention went back to the screen.

"John Baker is thought to have been the accomplice that escaped, and the search continues…" Nicki's voice wobbled slightly. "… And the attempted abductor, killed before he could leave the premises has been named… Christian Wood."

CHAPTER 25

My mind was whirling. Could this be true? I had to re-read the article from start to finish, twice, just to make sure. Everything he had told me had been a lie. Everything about watching over her, watching her children grow – was any of it true? Perhaps it had been, with a much darker undertone.

"There has to be some kind of mistake," I told Nicki as we got in the car. "Maybe the newspaper got the names wrong?" I wondered. It was possible, after all.

Nicki shook her head. "The newspaper had his parent's names in as well, father was called Henry, as was his son, I doubt that they would get that wrong. Emily, I know that you want to believe that he's a good guy, but he's lied to you about this, and goodness knows what else. I think you just need to confront him and tell him to get lost." She told me. I leant my head against the car window. There must be an explanation. Nicki stopped at the traffic lights and indicated to go right. I realised where she was going.

"Nicki, I can't go home! He'll be there, waiting for me. I need time to think!" I told her, panicking. The light turned green and Nicki hesitated.

"Where do you want to go?" She asked. I looked around wildly trying to gather my surroundings.

"Go straight on, to the park. We'll just park up and have a think," I said. I needed more time. Time to process, time to get things straight in my head. There must be a reason behind all of this. Maybe he just called himself Christian. But then why would you name yourself after the man that tried to kidnap your sister? Nothing made sense.

As Nicki pulled into the carpark I watched as children played on the nearby play equipment, enjoying the last rays of the Sunday warmth. "Damn, I've got a missed call from Jack, are you ok if I call him back?" Nicki asked.

"Yeah it's fine," I said as I continued to rest my head on the car window. Maybe it had been an honest mistake, and Christian hadn't been trying to kidnap her, and the newspaper got it wrong. But then, why didn't Christian just tell me his version of the story? Why try and make out that he was a different person completely?

"Hey Jack," I heard Nicki say. "Yeah Emily told me," A pause. "Yeah, I'm actually at the park with her now," She continued. "Yeah, we're just trying to figure something out at the moment." Another pause. "Oh, ok, yeah fine," She finished. "Bye," Nicki hung up the phone. "I think Jack is coming over here," She told me.

"Why?" I asked and she shrugged.

"I think he wants to help," She suggested. I tried not to roll my eyes.

"I don't think this is something he can help with." I sighed. "Nick... Do you think everything he's ever told me is a lie?" I asked her in a small voice, dreading to hear the potential truth.

"We can't know that for sure Em," Nicki hesitated. "For all we know, he was getting close to you and just lied about the story because he didn't want you to be afraid of him, or he didn't want you to judge him. Maybe underneath it all... Maybe he's still a good guy," Nicki said, but didn't seem convinced.

"Ok..." I said, slightly confused. "Now tell me what you really think."

Nicki sighed. "I think he's a bad guy, who got lucky by spotting a pretty girl who could see dead people, I think he thought of you as some kind of entertainment and now he thinks you might be a ticket out of here." Nicki finished.

I groaned. "Don't sit on the fence Nicki, tell me how you really feel," I muttered sarcastically.

"You asked," She shrugged. A moment later there was a tap on the window, I jumped, but it was only Jack.

"Care to take a walk?" He asked when I opened the door. I nodded and Nicki and I stepped out of the car, wandering down the path, away from the children's play area.

As we walked, Nicki filled in Jack with what had happened. I chipped in with some details, about how Christian had told me that he'd spent his time watching over Victoria, that by the time that she'd died and he wanted to be at peace with her but could no longer cross over.

"We've got to get rid of this guy," Jack exclaimed.

"I'm not sure it's as easy as that," Nicki told him. "It's not exactly like we can call the police and tell them that Emily has a stalker."

"There still might be an explanation to all this," I said feebly. The more we spoke about it, the more foolish I felt. He had told me I was special, watched over me, made me laugh, comforted me while I cried... Kissed me. Could it have all been some kind of act? To make me feel something for him, because he thought I could give him another shot at life? And what for? To try again, make something better of his life? Or so he could go back to abducting innocent girls? For a moment, I wished so badly that I could go back a month and be the girl whose only concern was levelling up on Candy Crush. How much had my life changed in such a short amount of time? How small my problems must have seemed then.

"I don't understand his end game here," Jack stated, confused. "If your Grams knows that he can't come back, then surely he knows it too? He's been around a lot longer." Jack contemplated.

"I think Christian is the only one that can answer that," I said, stopping. The area was secluded, and the sun was beginning to set. Was I ready to listen to them disparage Christian without even hearing him out first? This person that they were discussing, this man that I had read about in a paper, it wasn't the Christian that I knew. I reached up and pulled my necklace from my neck and dropped it to the floor. "Christian!" I called.

"Is that a good idea?" Jack asked, but I ignored him.

"Christian!" I called again. I needed answers, and he was the only one who could give them to me. I needed to know, one way or another, what was happening and who he really was.

Christian blinked into view in front of me. He looked from me, to Jack, then to Nicki.

"Do I want to know?" He asked, his face a little worried.

"He's here," I told Jack and Nicki. They moved a little closer to me. "Is Wood your surname?" I asked Christian directly. A flicker in his eyes was the only thing that gave him away, he kept his face perfectly still.

"What is this all about Emily?" He asked gruffly.

"Answer the question," I demanded. I would not be taken for a fool anymore.

Christian waited a moment looking back to Jack for a second. "It is," He confirmed through tight lips. A felt a shiver of cold sweep through me.

"I know the story about how you died is a lie." I told him. "I know you weren't Victoria's brother," I confirmed, almost choking on the words. There was no flash of surprise on Christian's face, nor no look of remorse.

"Can we discuss this somewhere private?" Christian asked through gritted teeth, his eyes flashing from Jack back to me.

"No, we can discuss this now. Are you not even going to try to deny it?" I asked, incredulous.

Christian sighed and pinched the bridge of his nose, like he had a headache coming. "Yes, ok I lied," He said quietly, shaking his head. "I know I should not have, and I'm sorry. You don't know how many times I wished I was the hero in the story, I so badly wanted to be the good guy for you," He insisted as he took a step towards me. "Let us go back home, I can explain everything," He lowered his voice, as if anyone could hear him. These are the words I had hoped he would say. I so badly wished that he could explain it all.

"Explain it to me here, now." I demanded.

"Don't let him talk you round," Nicki called to me and Christian flashed her an angry look. He quickly composed himself and looked back to me.

"I was in love," He began. "I courted Victoria, I thought she loved me too. Then Philip came into town… I do not know what he did to her, or what he said but the next thing that I know is that she is engaged to him… Like I was nothing. Like I *meant* nothing. I thought if I could get her away from him, away from everyone, for just one day, I could talk some sense into her. As you know… I never got that chance." He shook his head and looked at the ground.

My face was a mixture of disbelief and disgust. "You think that's what I want you to explain? Christian, I don't care who you were 100 years ago. I don't care what you did or why you did it. What I care about is who you are *right now*. And right now, all I see is a man who lied to me… and tells me some cock and bull story about love. God, you must think I'm such an idiot!" I yelled. His face fell.

"Do you not see though? Do you not understand? You are the spitting image of Victoria, like her in so many ways and more, this is our second chance, to make up for what happened, to be with each other, properly." He reached out for me, but I stepped away.

"You're wrong about that," I told him. "And I've been wrong about you." I shook my head and turned to leave. My world felt like it was crumbling.

"Is this because of him? Has he made you do this?" Christian called after me, pointing at Jack.

"No one can make me do anything Christian. He has nothing to do with this. I'm leaving now, don't follow me, don't come after me, don't hang around in my garden. Just go very far away." I told him sternly. I was too hurt, but I wouldn't cry, I would be strong.

"But we love each other," Christian said in a small, sad voice. "You told me that you would want to be with me, if there was a chance," He almost whispered, and I faltered in my stride. My heart ached for him.

"I'm afraid it's not possible," I said quietly. "I cannot create flesh and bone," I told him, and I carried on walking, I grabbed Jack and Nicki as I walked by them, who had been attempting to follow one half of the conversation.

"No," Christian called after me. "You cannot."

It happened so quickly, at first I wasn't sure what was happening. Time seemed to decelerate, and I saw everything in slow motion. Jack screamed and fell to his knees, clasping onto my hand, he pulled me down with him. On the other side of Jack was Christian, holding his other hand. His face was twisted in anger, almost unrecognisable. Christian screamed alongside Jack, both on their knees, their heads thrown back in pain. Nicki looked bewildered as she put herself in front of Jack, trying to find the cause of his pain. Jack was squeezing my hand now, tighter and tighter, I could not let go.

I felt the energy before I saw it. Like the throbbing pulse of a heartbeat making its way through my body and down my left hand, to Jack. I watched as the energy transferred to him, making his body convulse and causing him to scream louder. My throat tightened and I felt like I couldn't breathe. On my knees I watched as Christian placed his other hand over Jack's heart and a pulse of energy seemed to come from Christian, directly into Jack. A sort of energy exchange, but what did that mean? What could it do and why did I seem to be a part of it? I tried to wrench my hand away from Jack, but it was like steel, caught in his vice like grip. Jack seemed to slump lower as Christian towered over him, his hand over Jack's heart, pushing him down with every energy transfer.

"Jack!" Nicki had been yelling. "What's happening?!" She screamed at us both. My throat felt tighter still as my face contorted with the pain from my hand and the energy that was surging out of me.

"It's… Christian," I managed to splutter. Jack was nearing unconsciousness now and Christian's light seemed to be fading. All at once it seemed to dawn on me, what was happening and how I could stop it. Christian had never intended for me to re-create his body. He had always intended to take someone else's, but he couldn't do it alone.

"My necklace!" I shouted to Nicki over Christian's screams and I pointed behind me with my free hand. Nicki realised at once and scrambled behind me, her hands searching through the grass in the dark. Christian's screams were quietening now, and Jack was completely still. Energy was still flowing through me, slower now, but still there. Jack's vice grip hadn't lessened. "Nicki!" I shouted again. It felt like forever but could only have been seconds as Nicki ran back towards me.

"Here!" She said as she slammed the necklace into my free hand. With every ounce of strength that I could muster, I slammed my hand and the necklace onto Jack's chest. For a moment, nothing happened. Then time seemed to catch up with me as all at once Christian fell away from Jack and Jack released my hand. Christian grabbed at his hand that had been touching Jack protectively, like he had been burnt. He snarled like a wild animal and his amber eyes seemed to flash red. Christian seemed to be getting bigger and bigger, his body contorting and fading, before my eyes could adjust to what was happening, I felt him before I saw him. Through the dark I could see him for what he really was, I could feel the hatred in the air, bitter in my mouth. His body changed so much that he was no longer recognisable to me as Christian. His body was no longer a body, but instead, smoke and sludge.

CHAPTER 26

My heart sunk to my stomach as I realised the truth, my blood turned to ice as I stared at the disgusting form which was once Christian. My instinct was to run. Run away from the creature that still haunted my dreams. But Jack was still not moving.

"Grab the necklace Nicki," I told her quickly, I was still holding it against Jack's chest.

"What?" She asked, confused, she couldn't see what Christian had turned into.

"Grab it!" I shouted and Nicki scrambled to her knees as she placed her fingers around the stone.

Christian snarled again, louder this time, then all at once, like we weren't worth the trouble, Christian's smoke and sludge body seemed to melt into the ground, fading away, as if he had never been there. I let out a breath I hadn't realised I had been holding.

"I think we're safe for now," I told Nicki. "But just in case, don't let go of the necklace." I instructed her.

"How about Jack?" She asked. "Is he ok?"

I nodded though I wasn't sure. "It didn't work, so I think he's going to be ok," I said and leant over Jack to feel for a pulse. It was there, steady and strong. "Jack," I called, leaning over his body. Not daring to let go of the necklace. I tried shaking him slightly with my free hand. "Jack!" I called again, louder. Slowly, he began to stir, and his eyelids flickered. After a moment, he opened his eyes and tried to blink through the darkness.

"What happened?" He groaned as he tried to sit up.

"Long story," I told him. "But for now, we've got to get out of here," I tapped his arm and awkwardly, all three of us stood up and made our way to the car.

"Can you drive?" Nicki asked Jack after he climbed into the back seat. His car was parked just behind us.

"Yeah I think so," He nodded. "I'm feeling alright." I had managed to tell them both briefly what had happened with Christian.

"Jack, when do you start your new job?" I asked, seemingly out of the blue.

"Er, not for a couple of weeks, why?" He asked

"Nicki," I said, ignoring him. "What are the chances of you being able to call in sick for work tomorrow?" I asked.

Nicki smirked "As good as done," She told me.

"Good, I've got a plan, but for now, Jack, you've got to get away from me. It's not safe for us to be together, not while he's still around." I rummaged around in the bag I'd left in Nicki's car and found a pen and an old receipt. I scribbled down an address.

"Meet me here tomorrow, I'll text you a time. Don't say the address aloud," I instructed them.

With a nod, Jack got out of the car and headed for his own, then Nicki and I followed him out of the park.

Even though I still had the necklace, I practically ran inside my house and fell through the front door.

"Whoa, what happened to you?" Mum asked and I shot her a quizzical look.

"What do you mean?" I tried to ask innocently. Mum gestured at my appearance and I turned to look in the mirror. Bits of grass and dirt was in my hair and my jeans were covered in grass stains. "Would you believe me if I told you it's not what it looks like?" I asked. Mum raised an eyebrow.

"Do you want to tell me what's going on?" She asked and I slumped down on the sofa. I wasn't sure I had the energy.

"Do you remember that guy I told you about, the one that I said it wouldn't work with?" I asked and she nodded. "Well today I found out that he's been lying to me all along and not only that…" the words stuck in my throat as I pictured Christian in my mind, my beautiful Christian, as he turned into a monster of smoke and sludge. "He just wasn't who I thought he was," I whispered, a lump gathering in my throat.

"Oh Emily," Mum said as she sat down with me and started picking twigs out of my hair. "Boys are scum," she whispered as she leant her head against mine. After a moment, she asked: "What are you going to do?"

I was silent for a minute as I mulled over the words and the beginnings of a plan that was forming in my mind. A single tear escaped and rolled down my cheek.

"I'm going to move on," I told her.

*

I knocked on Angela's door the next morning, just before 10am. I'd managed to get in touch with her the night before and informed her it was urgent. She opened the door and quickly ushered me in.

"Oh Angela, I've been such an idiot," I told her once I was firmly seated on her purple sofa.

"What's happened then dear?" She asked as she poured the tea.

"Do you remember that bad spirit you felt, the one that had been bothering me?" I asked and she nodded, taking a sip from her teacup. "It turns out, he was masquerading as a friend. A nice spirit who I thought wanted to help me." I told her.

"Ah," Was all she said for a moment. "Seems he is a mischievous spirit." She said.

"No, I think it's a little worse than that. Yesterday, he tried to take over a friend of mine, tried to take over his spirit," I told her.

"But that's impossible," She quickly interjected.

"Yes, that's what I thought too." I told her. "He used me, somehow, used my energy or used my powers. I think through touching both me and him we were able to do some kind of energy transfer. I'm not sure I can explain it, it was more than a feeling if anything," I said, hoping that of all people, she would understand.

"And was he successful?" She asked, as if only mildly curious.

"No," I shook my head. "Actually, that was down to your necklace," I told her, and our heads spun to the front door as a loud knocked drummed from it. "…And we're going to need more." I told her as Angela got up to answer the door.

"Erm, hi, is our friend Emily here?" I heard Nicki ask.

"Yes, come through, come through," She called as she waved them into the lounge.

I put down my cup of tea and stood when they entered. "Angela, you might remember Nicki from the spirit group, and this is Jack, the unfortunate recipient of my spirit's attentions last night," I informed her.

"Cup of tea?" She asked, they shook their heads, but she went to gather teacups for them nonetheless.

Jack sat next to me on the sofa while Nicki crossed her legs on the rug in the middle of the room, staring around at the many fascinating objects around the room. Angela came back into the room with more teacups and settled herself on the armchair.

"Now, let's try this again from the beginning. Starting with who you really are… *Emily*," Angela looked over at me intently. Damn, I had hoped she hadn't noticed Nicki's slip at the front door.

I took a deep breath as I proceeded to tell her everything, from start to finish. I told her my full name and who I really was. I told her about what had happened at the night at the theatre, going into more detail than I had at the interview. I told her how it felt to see my colleague's dead on the floor, the feeling of being trapped when I had realised we couldn't open the gate lock. The horror of that night and how it stayed with me and probably always would. I then proceeded to tell her about the spirits I had met without realising they were spirits and how quickly I had become close to Christian.

Nicki and Jack listened without interruptions, both receiving new information that I kept from them both. Nicki's eyes widened in horror when I spoke about the kiss, but Jack just sat there in thoughtful contemplation.

"… and now we're here," I finished, downing the last dregs of my now cold tea.

Angela waited for a moment while the information sunk in. "Dear, it all sounds quite fascinating as well as terrifying, but I'm not exactly sure how I can help… or what it is you want me to do exactly. It sounds like you've got more power in you than I hold in my pinkie finger." She said and wiggled her pinkie at me.

"Firstly, I would like some more of these necklaces," I said, fingering my own. "I'm happy to buy them off you if you'd let me. Secondly, I'd like you talk me through it again. Tell me exactly how you banish someone to the Other Side."

CHAPTER 27

Back at my house, I glanced at my phone to check the time. It was now or never. Stepping out of the door I dialled Nicki's number. I had a quick glance around nervously.

"Hey, sorry to disturb you at work – but do you have the necklace?" I asked her, trying to appear as if I was keeping my voice down. "Dammit," I cursed after giving her a chance to respond. "It's got to be in the park somewhere still." I paused for a moment. "No, it's fine, I'll go look for it…. No don't worry, I doubt he'll be coming back anytime soon. Angela says they don't usually stay where they're not wanted," I paused again as I started walking down the road towards the park. "Yeah, it's fine, I'll call you after work. See you later," I hung up the phone and picked up my pace, shooting furtive glances around me. To a stranger looking in, it might look like I was trying not to be followed. Or at least, that's how I hoped it looked. I slowed down once I reached the gate to the park. With another glance over my shoulder, I closed the gate behind me and headed for the area that we'd been in only last night.

I spotted the area almost immediately, I eyed up a thin line of salt that was sprinkled on the ground and stepped over it into the secluded spot we had been in last night. The circle of salt would take up the area of a football field, enclosing the surrounding trees and the clearing we had struggling in last night.

I took my time scanning the floor, giving the appearance of searching for my necklace. I chewed my bottom lip, hoping to convey a look of concern. I did my best not to glance at the trees that surrounded me, trying not to give anything away. Another minute of looking and there was still no sign of Christian. Maybe my plan wasn't working, maybe he really had run off to lick his wounds. But from what Angela had told me, that isn't the way that spirits like Christian work. He was enjoying his time with me far too much to let me go just yet. Not without a fight.

I sighed heavily and dropped to my knees, searching through the grass with my fingertips, for a necklace that I knew wasn't there.

"Looking for something?" Christian appeared in front of me, back to his human form, a lazy smile on his face. My head snapped up as unbeknownst to him, he stepped inside my circle.

"What are you doing here?" I didn't have to fake the fear in my voice. Christian narrowed his eyes.

"I think you and I have some unfinished business," He smirked, flickering the hair away from his eyes.

"How dare you stand there and smirk at me," I stood, my anger real. "How dare you force your way into my life, pretend to care for me – like I'm some puppet made for your amusement," I scowled at him. *Don't look at the trees,* I told myself.

"Ah, you cannot pretend that you did not have fun as well. Caring for poor, old, lost soul Christian. Feeling special for once in your pathetic life. Feeling things you had only read about in books," His smirk turned into a snarl and he was no longer beautiful to me. Not now that I had seen his real face. Up until this moment, a small part of me had still wondered whether some of it had been real. The jokes that we had shared, the laughter, the intimate moments. Now I realised I really had been pathetic, bonding with a spirit I didn't know just because he made me feel special. Craving his attention, his love. Had my life really been so dull until the moment Christian came into my life, lighting it up so much that I fell for every murmured lie he told me? At least his venom made him easier to deal with now.

"I really did care about you Christian, for a moment there," I told him, keeping him talking and trying to hold his gaze. "But that doesn't make me pathetic. It makes me human. Which is more than I could ever say for you," I spat at him. "This is your last chance. Leave, and never come back here, otherwise you'll wish you had." I warned him, but it was merely words, I would never let him leave. There would never be a second chance. He barked a short laugh and took a step towards me, and I took a step back.

"No, I do not believe the fun is over yet," Christian's lip quirked upwards in a half mocking smile. I could barely believe the change in him, my brain could almost not recognise the person in front of me. My Christian wasn't mean, wasn't spiteful, wasn't cruel. But here is was. I almost wished he would keep up the pretence of caring for me, so I didn't have to taint my memory of him like this.

"No, you're right, it isn't." I shook my head sadly and through the corner of my eyes I saw him as he took another step towards me. "Now!" I shouted, and from behind the nearby trees, Nicki, Jack and Angela stepped out, removing their necklaces and raising their hands to the heavens, stepping inside the circle.

"Spirit lost, damned and died, we banish you to the Other Side," They all chanted in unison, walking towards me and Christian.

"I should have known you'd try something like this," He growled and took a step back. He waited a moment, trying to disappear over to his world and then froze, quickly discovering he couldn't leave. He looked around the park wildly as he tried to disappear but couldn't. As the others were getting closer, he began walking away from them, quickly, but found an invisible barrier outlining the area, he was trapped.

"Circle of salt," I told him, trying not to let my smugness show. "There was never a last chance to leave," I informed him casually as the others reached me and we all joined hands. "Spirit lost, damned and died, we banish you to the Other Side," I joined in. Christian's face had a fleeting moment of hatred as he casually backed off towards the other end of the circle, near the trees where he had first appeared.

"I would stop if I were you Emily," He called over to me, I glanced over to him whilst trying to keep my concentration, feeling the warmth of Nicki's and Angela's hands in mine. I watched as Christian reached behind a tree and pull something out. I dropped Nicki's and Angela's hands as I recognised what was in his hands. It was mum. Bound and gagged, she struggled against the invisible force that had restrained her, her blonde hair falling in front of her pale face. Panic shined in her eyes as she caught sight of me and struggled against the binds on her wrists. How in the world had he managed do to that? Christian wrapped his fingers around her throat. "Did you really think I would not have a backup plan?" He shouted to me, laughing manically. I stood up quickly and automatically went to her.

"Keep the circle," I shouted back towards my friends. Nicki watched me go with concern in her eyes, not being able to see what was happening behind her. "Let her go Christian, she has nothing to do with this," I snarled at him through gritted teeth, his hands still wrapped around her throat.

"Tell them to stop, unbind the circle, and I will let her go," He smiled sweetly. I hesitated and he squeezed her throat so hard that her eyes bulged, as if proving that he could do it. It didn't make sense to me. Christian couldn't even concentrate hard enough to turn the page of a book, how in the world did he have the power to do this?

Then it struck me. It really had been a lie, every last word. How many more things had he told me that wasn't true? Could he come into my house? My eyes narrowed. How trusting I had been, how stupid he must have thought of me as I sat and read to him.

"You son of a bitch," I shouted as I threw myself through the air and into the Inbetween, hitting him hands stretched into his chest, causing us both to fall onto the ground with a thud.

"Stupid girl," He scowled as he grabbed my shoulders and threw me to the floor, pining me down, I struggled beneath his weight. "Did you really think that I would have the strength to hurt her?" Christian laughed at me. "But with you, here, in the Inbetween, you're more ghost than girl. And that is something I *can* hurt," He laughed as he watched me struggle. "And while you're here, you have no power there, and let's face it, they will need your power to banish me." He scowled as he shoved me harder into the dark and I couldn't help but cry out in pain. This is what he wanted, to distract me, force me into the Inbetween where we would be on an even playing field.

Now invisible to my friends, unaware of the danger I was in, they continued holding hands and chanting together. Keeping to my plan as instructed. I didn't know how true Christian's words were, would three of them be enough to get rid of him? Angela had thought it might, but here is was, not fading away in the slightest. I had to get back to them and finish this off.

"All this time spent together Christian," I snarled as I struggled against his hands pinning me to the floor. "And you still don't know much about me, did you really think *I* wouldn't have a backup plan too?" I growled as I closed my eyes and took a deep breath. For a moment, everything went still, the shaking of my body calmed and the leaves blowing the wind seemed the quieten. With my mind I called out to them, pictured them in my mind, willing them to step forward now. Asking for their help. I felt the weight of Mary's ring on my finger, the smooth silk of Ben's tie against my chest, underneath my top, and Gram's necklace cool and solid against my throat. I opened my eyes just in time to see a large hand clamp down on Christian's shoulder as he was thrown away from me.

I sat up rapidly as I watched Mary, Grams and Ben gather around Christian, like my own miniature army. Ben grabbed Christian's arms and locked them behind his back, and he struggled with him as he pushed him forwards, closer to the circle. Christian might be stronger in my world, but in the Inbetween it was anyone's game. I immediately ran towards mum and ripped the tape from her mouth. "I can't explain now, but it's almost over," I told her hurriedly, glancing down at the ropes that bound her, I wouldn't even know where to start and there was no time. I gave her arm a brief squeeze as I ran back towards Nicki and grabbed her and Angela's hands.

"Spirit lost, damned and died, we banish you to the Other Side," We all chanted together. Angela had said the words didn't matter too much, it was more about the meaning behind them, the joined life force all wanting the same thing. But a rhyming chant just felt more powerful to me.

I could feel the energy again, but not like last night, which was harsh and forced and painful. This instead felt powerful and calming at the same time. I watched as energy spread from my body to theirs and vice versa, spreading together and merging, becoming one. I looked towards the spirits, as Ben held Christian tightly in his grip and Grams and Mary stood either side, Grams should have looked small and frail, but she didn't, she looked formidable to me, they all did. Christian, still struggling, locked eyes with me, his eyes narrowing, anger spilling from them. I held his gaze for a moment, no longer afraid and no longer entranced by those eyes. He had lost all power over me, for once, I really was the one in control. I watched as he became weaker, so weak he no longer struggled against Ben's grip and his gaze slipped from mine. I let the chant die on my lips.

"It's time to let go Christian," I told him as the others carried on with the chant. Angela had explained this would be painful for him, ripping him away from the Inbetween that had become his home. Sending him reluctantly to the Other Side, where he belonged, whether he accepted that or not.

"You can't make me," Christian growled but his voice seemed weak, the fight had left him despite his words. His face contorted in pain for a moment as he winced, and for a moment I saw a glimpse of the spirit I had got to know and came to care for. Even though he had turned out to be manipulating and malevolent, he had still helped me gain a better control over my new power and taught me to embrace it rather than fear it. And for that Christian, who perhaps existed somewhere inside of him, I hoped he could find peace.

I gave him a half smile. "Goodbye Christian," I whispered and with panic in his eyes, he began to fade away.

CHAPTER 28

"Right everyone! I would like to re-introduce back to the group – Emily! Formerly known as Emma," Frankie laughed. I was greeted with hellos and a small cheer from Angela.

"And this is my mum," I said pointing towards her. "She just wants to get a chance to see what it is you do here," I explained as we found seats in the circle. Mum waved a little nervously.

It had been a few months since I had unbound her from the ties that Christian had put her in and explained to her from start to finish about exactly what had been going on. Luckily, there was no choice but for her to believe it, considering what had happened to her and what she had seen.

"We're going to start with a meditation," Frankie declared as she told us how to breathe. I let the sound of her soothing voice calm me.

I had continued with my learning with Angela, who had asked me to come back to the spirit group to see if I could get anything further out of that. I had hoped bringing mum along could help her understand a little more about what it was that I was doing and what I was going through. She was understanding, as I knew she would be, but I think it would be a while before she really came to terms with it.

"Ok, everyone, we've got some tipping tables here, I would like four to a table," Frankie asked as we all stood up.

"How does it work?" I asked, intrigued.

"You all put your hands on the table, one side is marked yes and one side no, you ask the spirits a question and their energy will tip the table in the direction of the answer," Frankie informed me.

We all gathered around the tables. "Are there any spirits here present?" Asked a woman on my table, after a moment, the table tipped slightly towards 'Yes'. Mum's eyes widened in alarm.

"Are there?" She whispered to me. An elderly gentleman to the left of me laughed delicately as he placed his hand on the table, he had the unmistakable glowing aura around him that I was coming to recognise.

"Yes," I whispered to mum. "There certainly are."

Printed in Great Britain
by Amazon